FAMILY MYTHS AND LEGENDS

PATRICIA FERGUSON

PENGUIN BOOKS

Penguin Books Ltd, Harmondsworth, Middlesex, England
Viking Penguin Inc., 40 West 23rd Street, New York, New York 10010, U.S.A.
Penguin Books Australia Ltd, Ringwood, Victoria, Australia
Penguin Books Canada Limited, 2801 John Street, Markham, Ontario, Canada L3R 1B4
Penguin Books (N.Z.) Ltd, 182–190 Wairau Road, Auckland 10, New Zealand

First published by André Deutsch Ltd, 1985
Published in Penguin Books 1986

Made and printed in Great Britain by
Richard Clay (The Chaucer Press) Ltd,
Bungay, Suffolk
Filmset in Monophoto Plantin by
Northumberland Press Ltd, Gateshead,
Tyne and Wear

J. Wyger Wardingley Nardro 1987

Penguin Books

FAMILY MYTHS
AND LEGENDS

Patricia Ferguson took an arts degree at Leeds University, then trained as a nurse and a midwife. She lived in Canada for some time, but is now in London where she is writing and working as a nurse. *Family Myths and Legends* is her first novel.

FOR MY PARENTS

ONE

JOAN stood in the kitchen, contemplating a murder. With her small puffed hands she was making a pot of tea: filling the kettle, lighting the gas, rinsing the pot. Inside she was Lady Macbeth, and giving herself a good talking-to.

One ampoule would do. Double the Nitrazepam, still within the normal limits if anyone ever thought to check. And when the old bag's out cold, pop the needle into a vein and Bob's your – no. No, too risky. Thin ancient veins, once breached, ooze, spreading eloquent bruises beneath the skin. Besides, the old bag was fat; it would be hard to raise a decent vein from under all the padding.

It would need to be muscle, then. Get her on her side when she's settling for the night. Prop her there with pillows. Whisper from the doorway,

'All right, Mum?'

And when the answer was a snore, tiptoe within, raise the bedclothes, lift the nightdress, swab the area, Upper-and-Outer-Quadrant-of-the-Buttock, and –

No, again. Why bother to swab the area at a time like that? Joan's evil subconscious, sidetracked, remembered a joke seen long ago on television: man about to be shot, officer asks him if he'd like a cigarette, man replies, No thanks, I'm trying to give it up.

Joan laughed to herself softly, and saw that the kettle had boiled. Joan filled the teapot. 'A quick spurt, then slowly fill to the top.' She had read these instructions in a magazine article just after the War, and memory has read them out to her at tea-making ever since.

'Tea-tray,' cried Joan aloud, as she put the kettle down. It was a call for attention. 'Tea-tray!' as a toast-master might quiet a hubbub of conversation before the main speeches.

'Tea-tray!' On the third repetition Joan heard herself, remembered where she was and what she was doing, looked about her and found the ready-laden tea-tray standing in front of her on the kitchen table. She checked it over. Two cups, two saucers, plate of censored biscuits – nearly all of the slightly less fattening variety – and a bottle of sterilized milk.

'All set –'

Now that winter was coming the passage had somehow recovered its old smell, Joan noticed as she climbed the short flight of stairs to the living-room. She sniffed, concentrating, and thought of her father's last dog, and of her father's wrinkled hand-made roll-ups. Perhaps it was her father's ghost, then, that lurked here in the dark passage; it would be just like him to haunt the earth merely as a smell. Poor old boy.

Joan shouldered the living-room door open.

'Here we are.'

Majestic Lily turned to stare. She had left her teeth out today and her top lip, pushed upward by her lower jaw, was squashed against her nostrils so that her breathing whistled loudly and fluttered, as if she had just been out for a quick run or violently lost her temper. She lay piled in her armchair like a heap of small rubber tyres. She wore a floral cross-over apron, of the sort worn by charladies in cartoons.

She eyed the biscuits with a calm carnivorous gleam, as if they were a plateful of tender young mice and she a ravening owl.

'There.' Joan laid the tea-tray down on the little table beside her mother.

Lily, her eyes on the tea-things, continued to whistle and snort. Joan remembered a wildlife programme on the television, which had showed close-ups of languid bristly walruses stretched out beside the rolling sea.

'What are you laughing at, might I ask?'

'Didn't know I was,' said Joan guiltily.

'Grinning like an ape,' said Lily with vigour. 'Who you got in there anyway?'

'What?' For a moment Lady Macbeth peeped out anxiously through the curtains, then whisked herself away again.

'You heard,' said Lily slyly. 'Who you got out there in the kitchen?'

Joan grinned helplessly.

'I heard you talking in there, laughing. What you up to? At your age.'

'Honestly, Mum –'

'You ain't got no man in there? Aw, thought you'd got a man in there. Thought there was something going on at last.'

Joan poured out the tea, feeling obscurely relieved.

'Those coconut?'

So now she's hearing things, thought Joan as she handed the plate. Hearing voices. Wasn't that the first sign of madness? Joan felt a warm spark of pleasure at the idea. First sign of madness. Or was that talking to yourself?

Lily's voice broke in on these thoughts before they could turn any worrying corners.

'What time is it?' Chin steeply lowered, she was dabbing up the crumbs on her bosom, fingering them one by one between her lips.

Clock's just behind you, thought Joan smartly as she turned the television on.

'Turn it up a bit.' Joan sighed very loudly before rising again.

'May as well draw the curtains while I'm up,' she remarked briskly. Lily did not look up from the screen. Joan wandered over to the window and stood staring out of it. She could see the pale October sky through the holes in the roof opposite. The Fulljames's house had been bricked up already, doors and windows blocked with raw new bricks. Supposing someone had been left inside by accident? Suppose, thought Joan, some poor tramp had woken to find himself walled up alive, and was even now tearing at the cement with bleeding finger-nails?

Lily glanced up: the adverts had come on. Joan was still standing by the window, mooning as usual. It was Joan's legs that infuriated Lily and always had; the way she stood, with her stomach stuck out and her calves bowed outwards. It was the backward-curving calves, thought Lily, more than anything else. Her calves and her limp wondering expression, as if she had just asked someone a polite question, inquired after someone's health perhaps, and was waiting nicely for the answer. It was aggravating, Lily thought. It got on Lily's nerves. Lily sighed too, and went back to the film.

Joan drew the curtains, and presently, back in her own armchair, joined Lily in the flickering blacks and whites, aware of that growing inner silence she had long thought of as tranquillity.

Time passed, marked by sets of adverts. The old house grew an evening older. In the roof, joists moved in immeasurably small ways, as the wind blew harder, and on the top storey the doors of all the empty bedrooms vibrated in their frames. Into one cold fireplace a little ancient soot fell.

In the kitchen shadows moved, and a mouse broke cover.

The curtained alcove beneath the sink was a playground for mice. There were leaning towers of shoe-polish tins, stumps of candle, many aromatic boxes of cleaning powders, some quite bent with damp old age, and certain articles of under-wear put by for thrifty use as dusters and still sporting a button here and there, or an eloquent sag of elastic; and above all there rose a strong soupy smell, ambrosial to mice, from the floorcloth slung stiffening in the curve of the S-bend.

In the bright warm living-room Lily fell asleep, and the music of the suspense film on television entered her dreams and soured them unpleasantly. She was crouching at the foot of the stairs, trying to wrap some parcels. The task was difficult because the presents refused to lie still and submit to being wrapped. Wriggling like hooked eels they fought her hands as she caught the edges of the wrapping paper together and struggled to tie imprisoning knots in the string. Lily began to cry with vexation, because the parcels must be wrapped soon, or disaster, something large with heavy boots on, would overtake her. 'Please, please,' wept Lily, but the presents took no notice, merely struggling all the more as if to mock her.

In desperation Lily caught up a hammer and began to beat at the presents with it. The hammer-head sank and sprang up as if she was battering living, resilient flesh, but Lily in terror was merciless, and hammered on until the presents lay still and she knew that they were dead. She had killed them! Whimpering, Lily took a corner of the wrapping-paper between finger and thumb, and gingerly lifted it to look at what lay dead beneath.

'You all right, Mum?'

Lily found herself gasping in her own chair by the gas fire, opposite daft Joanie, whose cheek, as usual, was swollen about some bon-bon, and in whose eyes, for an instant, Lily noticed a quite unfamiliar expression.

'You screamed, Mum!' Joan sounded rather impressed,

as if her own nightmares never came close to achieving such dramatic audience responses, and she felt the loser thereby.

'Mum?' Joan rattled the bon-bon around her front teeth from one side of her mouth to the other.

Lily, breathing more easily, scanned her own mind, but like an enemy submarine the dream was quietly submerging. It was a dream about string, about fish, she had been young again and slender – the submarine vanished, leaving only ripples on the water to mark its passage.

Joan got up, her toffee wedged into one side of her mouth for storage during speech, and said rather loudly,

'Are you feelin' all right, Mum?'

'Just dreaming. A nightmare, thass all.'

'Best get off to bed, then?'

'Stop that yelling, I ain't deaf.' Lily's tone was still subdued. She was embarrassed. Only children screamed at nightmares, or villains in films when their evil pasts caught up with them.

'I told you you can't eat cheese. I don't know, you never listen to me, it always upsets you.' It wasn't often that Lily looked beaten. Joan pressed her advantage. 'Don't you think you ought to be in bed?'

Lily pretended that her acquiescence was purely coincidental. 'Give us a hand up, eh, gel?' Her face was bland; Joan was checked.

'That's just what I've been telling you,' she muttered. She lengthened her stance, bent at the knees, and heaved at Lily's elbow while Lily pushed against the armchair on the other side.

'Stick.'

'Here.'

Lily cautiously straightened her back, which she had curled forwards for balance. Look how many feet you need when you get old, she thought. This stick and Joanie, that's five, I need five feet to get about on. Nearly a bluebottle's worth of feet just to get up to bed with.

'Don't you ever get this old,' she sighed to Joan as they manoeuvred around the armchair. They moved in halting rushes and swerves, as if they were a crowd, the two of them.

'I won't,' replied Joan, remembering that when Lily had been as old as she, Joan, was now, her eldest daughter had already left work to come and look after her. Who'd look after me, if I got to be as old as she is? No one, that's who. No bloody one, thought Joan, feeling very grown-up.

'I won't,' she repeated, as they neared the stairs.

'Stop a minute.'

Joan looked quickly about the floor. 'What, mice?'

'Just wait a minute, will you,' cried Lily irritably. The dream-submarine had re-surfaced. Something to do with the stairs, with fish, with string? The periscope was lowered again with a last derisory wink. Presents?

Lily shook her head. 'All right.'

'One at a time then,' said Joan as usual. 'And . . . up! And . . . up! And . . . up!'

Lily fell down these stairs once, in 1924, but seemed none the worse for it. Joan's little sisters screamed down the last curl of these stairs on a metal tea-tray, both whooping with fearful laughter; and once Jimmy rode the winding bannister all the way down from the third floor to the dark ground-floor passage, and bent a little bone in his right forearm when forced to crash-land at the bottom.

'And . . . up! And . . . made it!'

Across the landing – push wide the door – flick the switch. Each line of the flooring under the lino, each slight give of old wood beneath the soles, as familiar as breathing. There were the two Chinese vases on either side of the heavy bevelled dressing-table mirror; there was the bed, sagging on the side that had been Lily's when her husband staked his small claim on the other.

'Steady?'

'Mm.'

'Give us your arm then.'

Sometimes Lily seemed too tired to stretch out her arms and legs to help with the undressing. Sometimes it was quite a nasty struggle to get her things off, a show of unseemly violence (Joan had occasionally thought, imagining disgusted spectators) between two ageing ladies.

Tonight Lily was co-operative.

'Got it?'

'No ... just a minute. There, bend your head ... right. Now this arm –'

Lily lay in bed, meekly shrouded in blue winceyette. Joan tucked her in. She enjoyed putting her mother to bed.

'Call me if you want anything, all right?'

'G'night darling,' said Lily tenderly from her pillows. She often felt quite affectionate towards Joan at bedtime. It was cosy to be tucked into bed, and somehow less chafing to be helpless at night.

'Dunno what I'd do without you,' said Lily.

'Oh there,' snapped Joan, pleased and infuriated. She crossed the room to the fireplace, which seemed to exude coldness as fireplaces will where there is no fire, and tested the mantelpiece for dust with her forefinger.

Lily's praises, when they came, filled her always with an unpleasant emotion, which she felt in her intestines, an uncomfortable heaviness as indigestible as Christmas dinner.

The forefinger showed a grey oval of dust. Joan pulled a handkerchief out from the sleeve of her cardigan, where it had bulged and loosened the material over her wrist, and scrubbed away at the mantel. She wondered what it was that she felt, this intestinal emotion. Perhaps other people, feeling it, would be able to translate it into words, use it as a weapon or as a candle in the dark. Other people, not people like me, Joan concluded. The emotion, as ever, lay beyond her reach, sensed but unidentifiable. Joan made a practised effort, rather like swallowing to order, and ignored the feeling until it went away.

She tucked her grimy handkerchief back into its hiding place.

'N'night then.'

Lily gave her a smile, sweet and lavish, a bedtime smile. 'Sweet dreams,' she said.

For a minute Lily sat quite still in the bed, listening to the diminishing stair-creaks of Joan's descent, until the suspense film, now at the urgent-violins stage, was abruptly muffled by the closing of the living-room door. Then she leant over towards the bedside table, selected a hairgrip from amongst the crusted trio littered beside her hairbrush, and tenderly inserted the looped end into her right ear, turning it delicately to dredge for wax.

Tonight the haul was disappointing. She tried the other ear, and at length captured a little hard golden crumb, which she turned meditatively between her fingers for a moment or two before flicking it beneath the bed.

What was I dreaming about down there, Lily wondered. She remembered her pounding heart, and the uncomfortable notion of parcels which had assailed her at the foot of the stairs. But no further trace of the dream chose to resurface.

Lily replaced the hairgrip and turned out the light. She sat up to sleep lately or she dreamt of suffocation, and woke breathless as if real water had seeped into her lungs as she slept.

'You should see a doctor,' Joan had worriedly told her several times over the past few months. 'Find out what's doing it.'

Lily had been scornful. 'Bloody hell, girl, I *know* what's doing it, don't I? I'm bloody eighty-*six*, aren't I? I don't need no bleeding doctor to tell me that.'

Joan had turned away at that, her anxiety distracted into simple annoyance, because both of them knew that Lily was only eighty-four. Stands to reason, thought Lily in the darkness as her eyes closed. If it was that important a dream, those parcels, I wouldn't have forgotten it.

In her own room later that night, after she had read aloud the gas stove ('OFF OFF OFF OFF') and re-checked the doors, Joan opened the bottom drawer of her dressing-table and took out a shoebox. This she carried to the small table by the curtained window, and set beside the glass aquarium where two goldfish quietly revolved.

'Well now,' said Joan conversationally to the fish, 'what shall we have today?' Through their thin fronds of water-weed the goldfish floated dispassionately, like birds sus-pended in slow-motion flight, birds in a strangely contained volume of thickened air. In one corner of the tank, its feet embedded in the coloured gravel, stood a miniature table of white plastic, with two little chairs to match.

'Didn't you like it?' Joan breathed a secret laugh. Neither fish seemed to have shown any inclination to be seated.

'Suit yourselves then.' Gliding one hand into the cold water Joan pulled out the furniture, slowly, so as not to frighten anybody.

'Get off, you.' She flicked with her fingernail at a small brown snail which had glued itself to the table's underside. 'Nasty little slimy thing.' The snail plipped back into the water, turned heavily once in the underwater version of spinning, and rocked itself to rest amid the gravel. 'Not for the likes of you . . .'

Joan took the lid off the shoebox, and with one hand whiffled the tissue paper about inside. The box was full of tiny pieces of furniture, of several varieties, from the stark, rather Scandinavian lines of the white plastic kitchen goods to the miniature china baroque of heavy hall-stands and wardrobes garlanded with painted flowers.

Furniture, Joan had discovered, converts space into

rooms. Give the fish an oven, and they lived happily enough in a drowned kitchen; substitute a sofa and they swam no less content in a submerged drawing-room.

Joan had developed a taste for the white plastic, which she felt showed the cool, classic lines a fish might be expected to prefer. But tonight, she thought, the fish deserved a change. A new acquisition, no less, and one smuggled out of the shop under the assistant's very nose; one snaffled, pocketed, pinched, wogged, nicked. Shop-lifted.

'Heh heh!' Joan held up her latest prize, a small black model of a television set, with a plastic picture of two cowboys on the little screen. When she tilted the set to and fro and squinted slightly, Joan could see the nearer cowboy shoot his gun at the other, who at that instant flung himself jerkily to the ground and stretched himself out flat, clearly dead.

Joan carefully poked the set into the gravel at one corner of the aquarium. 'I don't know if you can get BBC 2.' She laughed again, quite loudly. 'But you can always try.' Joan thought of the goldfish twiddling helplessly at the little knobs with their filmy golden fins, and gently bumping their perplexed noses against the screen. She sat down on her bed, her arms folded, rocking herself back and forth and laughing in painful gulps.

A sudden wet, racketing snore arrested her in mid-hoot. Sitting curved on the bed she held her breath and listened. Eventually another snore came, then another. Joan uncurled and stood up.

'Ssh!' she whispered to the fish, her fingers at her lips, 'She's asleep.' Quickly she undressed, piling her clothes untidily on the chair beside the bed. Then she seized her nightdress-case poodle by the ears and jerked it briefly into life by unzipping and disembowelling it of her own pink nylon nightdress. Wearing this she bundled the shoebox together and stuffed it back into the dressing-table drawer, pulling a woollen jumper over it for extra camouflage.

For a moment before climbing into bed, Joan watched the aquarium. The bigger of the two fish was hovering in front of the television set, this latest invasion. He seemed to be inspecting it, his translucent nose half an inch from the screen, while his tail moved slowly, unsurprised, in the cold water of his new lounge.

Joan lay down, the empty poodle agape beside her, and began the long wait for sleep, still smiling.

TWO

CISSIE arrived at three the next day. She stood on the steps stout and solid like a little well-lagged boiler on two short legs, her arms held out at wide angles to accommodate the bunched plastic carrier bags in either hand.

'Sorry I'm late and all that, am I coming in or what?'

Joan backed accordingly.

'You're not looking well,' Cissie said in the half-light of the passage. 'What you been doing to yourself? You off this afternoon? Here, take this, will you? What a day. Went up Oxford Street. See this? A man done that, coming out of Selfridges. Suitcase. Didn't half hop. Where's Mum?'

'In the living-room.' Joan turned to look in the hall-stand mirror. 'How d'you mean, not well?' But Cissie had already disappeared. Joan looked again at her own image, gave herself a faint inflection of the eyes, a swift private bulge of complicity. Out soon anyway, she told her reflection.

In the living-room Cissie had pulled the two armchairs closer together.

'See this? My material for my dress.' She hauled up a swag of deep blue cloth. 'See them. Peacocks.' She held a fold of it to her own round cheerful face. 'What you think, suit me?'

'Very nice,' said Lily, fingering the stuff. It was damply silky to the touch.

'Lovely,' said Joan.

'You see the pattern, it's got those whatsits, panels, what d'you call them? Something panels off of the shoulders anyway. And blue shoes and a handbag. No gloves, I said to her, to Marion, I said, You don't wear gloves these days. You got a hat, Joan? I've got to get the hat. Blue, or white as a contrast, what d'you think?'

The doorbell interrupted her.

'That's your friend then,' said Cissie, her eyes meeting Lily's. She poked her tongue quickly into one cheek and looked down, silent.

Joan rose perplexedly. Why was it so? she wondered. Why was her recent friendship with a woman of similar background to herself somehow a joke? But then all Joan's small adventures in friendship had been a joke to Cissie, and to Lily too. Years before when she had met a young man or two Lily and Cissie had teased her about it for months afterwards.

The trouble with me is, thought Joan as she went to the front door again, is that when people tease me, I can't help but listen. When Cissie laughed at that Henry because his ears stuck out, I felt too embarrassed to be seen about with him, I told him I didn't want to see him again. And then look what Cissie married! Her Jeff's ears would've won prizes over that Henry's. I said so at the time, didn't I? Didn't seem to bother Cissie though, my saying it, if I *did* say it . . .

On the other hand, maybe Cissie was right about Dierdre. Maybe she and Mum were right to laugh. Dierdre *is* odd, people will think I'm odd too for knowing her, I don't really like her anyway, oh dear –

Joan opened the front door again. Instead of standing perkily on the steps as Cissie had, Dierdre, clad as usual in her thick creased sheepskin jacket, lounged against the low wall which once, before the First World War, had been topped with a fence of iron railings. One of Dierdre's round laced-up shoes idled in the dust between the worn-down iron stumps which were all that a grateful government had left behind.

'Hallo, Dierdre.'

'Hi. All set?' Dierdre liked an abrupt and military tone.

'Er, no, just a minute, get my coat on –'

Carefully Joan pushed the door to until it was nearly shut. She did not want Dierdre to think of stepping inside. It didn't seem safe to let Dierdre too far into the house. Joan ran upstairs to get her coat, thinking as she did so that she could have said to Dierdre, as she'd pushed the door to, 'I won't keep you a moment.'

That was it; with a nice gracious smile too. Won't keep you a moment. It was enough to make you imagine, thought Joan at the wardrobe, that social poise was simply a question of remembering other people's lines. Confident types remembered other people's lines, and said graciously, I won't keep you a moment.

No, decided Joan, shaking her head at her reflection in the hall-stand mirror, no, surely it can't be as simple as all that.

She ducked into the living-room, and was immediately conscious of avid conversation abruptly broken off. There seemed still a hum in the air.

'I'm off then,' she said weakly into this hum.

'Right you are,' replied Cissie affably.

'You won't forget her tablets?'

'Mum'll remind me if I do,' said Cissie meaningly. She disapproved of what she thought of as Joan's mollycoddling of Lily: making an invalid out of her, that's all it was, to make herself feel needed, poor thing, well who could blame her come to think of it?

'She still stood out there?' asked Cissie, having reached

the end of the mental spool of tape which the sight of Joan always clicked to ON.

'We're off now.'

'Bubbye then.'

'See you,' smirked Lily.

Joan closed the door and raced back along the passage, snatching up her handbag on the way.

'Here I am.'

Dierdre swaggered still against the stumps of railings, her profile turned into the wind.

'Think it looks like rain?' She turned her great head like a permed St Bernard to face her friend. 'Want to take the car?'

'Oh, yes, I think so,' agreed Joan, who loved rides in cars, since she had so few.

In the Datsun, edging out into the traffic of the main road, Dierdre began a long monologue about the knocking noise in the front right wheel, and how it might well be the bearings.

Joan, happy in her seatbelt, considered bearings and soon lost track of Dierdre's tale. Bearings. Could such a vague and medieval-sounding word really refer to a tangible piece of modern machinery? What would a Bearing do when it aged, would it pry loose, or rust, or suddenly bend? There were other such vague and plural words, too. Holdings, for example. Holdings. He had extensive holdings in –

'Forty-seven pounds!' Dierdre shouted suddenly. She smacked the steering wheel with her large hand. She wore a ring on the middle finger of her left hand, a heavy gold snake swallowing its own tail.

'Tch tch,' said Joan, wondering whether Dierdre meant money or fat, 'dear me.'

'Exactly,' cried Dierdre excitedly. 'That's what I told him. You think you're going to get that sort of money out of me, my lad, well, I told him, fat chance!' She struck the wheel again. 'Fat chance!'

'Look, there's one,' said Joan, who had noticed where they were.

'Too small. This isn't a Mini, you know.'

'There!'

'Too late, can't turn.'

'Over there?'

'Never driven, that's your trouble. Always chauffeured about, that's you. Here we go, here we go. Right. Lock the door, won't you. D'you know how many cars are stolen in London every day?'

'What they do there anyway, at the museum?' Cissie wondered aloud, as she ran the hot water into the sink. She noticed as she did so a small bubble, like a green plastic blister, in the bottom of the washing-up bowl, and began cautiously to pull at it with her finger- and thumb-nails.

Lily shrugged, to convey her lack of interest. Since she knew Cissie's opinion of Joan's ministrations to herself, Lily was a rather different woman when Cissie was visiting; a plucky old lady, one who resisted her eldest daughter's stifling attentions as far as kindness allowed, and accepted what remained with resignation.

This was not always an easy part to play, as appearances had to be kept up on occasional fortnights at Cissie's own house; though there Lily's room was on the ground floor, where there was also an extra toilet. Even so the exhaustion ensuing from these fortnights of independence meant that Joan would be forced to wait even more closely on her mother when Lily returned to her own home. Which on the whole was worth the trouble, in Lily's eyes, since Cissie invariably telephoned for a health report during Lily's first week at home.

'Oh, she's terrible,' Joan would wail. 'She can't hardly eat without me feeding her, she can't get her slippers off by herself even –'

And Cissie, who heard accusation in these words, and who had watched Lily coping admirably all by herself for a fortnight, would inevitably reach simmering point, and her next visits to Lily and Joan would be interestingly punctuated with long rows and beratings. During the rows Lily might play peacemaker, trying to reconcile her warring daughters with soft maternal guidance; or she might, on the other hand, egg one on against the other as the mood took her.

Far more interesting and complicated were the rows which also involved Jessie, who tended to swop sides between Joan and Cissie, and whose allegiance to either was always based on terms known only to herself, so that which side she was on always came as a surprise.

Today Lily wanted some gossip; she wanted to let herself go with a little malice. She was not interested in Joan's outings.

'Gets her out of the house,' she conceded.

'Yeah. But looking at dollshouses. At their age,' said Cissie. Cissie had pierced the skin of the blister now. She pulled delicately, her finger and thumb as tweezers, and detached a limp shred of green plastic skin like a little piece of lettuce leaf. She discarded it on the draining board and scratched at the roughened perimeter of the blister with her fingernail, trying to catch another edge. None arose, so she laid the bowl flat and began to run hot water into it.

'Can't see her nursing, that Dierdre,' Cissie went on, as she squirted in a yellow dart of washing-up liquid. 'Can't see her soothing any fevered brows.'

'She did the linens, Joan said, linens or something. You know, counting piller-cases, something like that,' said Lily, scenting an opening but unable to follow it up; what little Joan knew about Dierdre had been extracted and passed on and mulled over several months before.

'Wool, told you then, that's not proper nursing is it? Not like Joan.'

Lily remembered something: a mild enough snippet but the best she could do under the circumstances.

'I told Jessie about it, them and the dollshouses, and you know what she says?'

'Tell me.'

'Wool, she says, "I expect they're just checking, see, to make sure nobody's *moved*."'

'They just never get the curtains right,' said Dierdre bitterly, as she stirred her tea.

'Too heavy,' agreed Joan comfortably. She was sitting in her favourite seat, right beside the window so that she could look out through the café's orange net at the passing shoppers, the women with pushchairs and untidy hair, the women with umbrellas and raincoats and the wrong sort of shoes on. Joan could easily spot mistakes in other people's clothes, and often wondered why she could never apply this stylish accuracy to her own.

'It looks like carpet,' continued Dierdre fretfully, 'as if you and I had hung our windows with great strips of carpet.'

Joan watched two young girls, both stocky and crop-haired, walk soberly past in tight split-sided skirts and plimsolls. She enjoyed them, marvelling, until they had disappeared round the corner and then offered: 'Wonder if they could use crêpe de chine?'

'Could do, could do,' Dierdre considered, fingers in her thick doggy grey curls. 'Like heavy satin in scale, d'you think?'

'It used to be quite cheap. Used to be underwear, when you made your own. When I was in my teens.'

It was a daring confidence. Dierdre looked a little disconcerted. Clearly crêpe de chine had never figured in her own wardrobe, teenage or no. Joan was pleased at this, feeling that she had seen more of Life than Dierdre had.

'If they used, you know, the darker colours,' said Dierdre tentatively.

Joan nodded. Clearly they couldn't use the pale pastels of lingerie. She looked out of the window again. She would have liked to ask Dierdre who 'they' were. But Dierdre would have been embarrassed at the question, or at any rate would have appeared so; she preferred to pretend that she meant the museum-curators, or perhaps she really did mean them, Joan thought. Whereas Joan herself, during these critical talks over tea, referred entirely to the dollshouses' inhabitants, discussing the difficulties of miniature house-wifery as if being two inches high were a common domestic problem, on a par with entertaining in a bedsit or cooking elegant meals for one. Moreover, Joan thought in particular of the servants' hall. In the Gate Baby House, a miniature Georgian wonder and Joan's favourite, an evident parlour-maid waited stolidly in one corner of the panelled dining-room, wearing a faded mob cap and Edwardian curves. There was something in the pursed waxen face and folded arms that spoke to Joan of hard service unquestioningly rendered, of the old-time servants who knew their place. Knowing your place was a comforting notion to Joan, who had always known her own. In Joan's imagination the Gate House's little maids, when the museum was dark and empty of larger human life, stealthily wielded feather dusters and wash-leathers, and polished up the fire irons and blackened the kitchen range.

It was strange, thought Joan, picking up her teacup, that she simply could not see the Gate House Master and Mistress, who wore evening dress in the first-floor drawing-room, as anything but dolls, a couple of tiny wax dummies, limp in armchairs, or slumped as if drugged over the grand piano. As if only hard work brought you to life. Well, there might be something in that, thought Joan.

'Or they could dye it,' Dierdre said at last.

Joan saw the buxom waxen tweenies boiling up a thimble-

26

sized copper full of dye on the range while completing their other evening duties: briskly dusting down the Master, perhaps, or hauling his lady wife into her carpeted four-poster for the night.

'Yes. I suppose they could.'

'Did you see that Japanese doll?' asked Dierdre suddenly. 'Special Exhibition. Its face was made of crushed oyster shells.' She touched her own battered cheek rather dreamily. 'Just imagine.'

Joan tried obediently to imagine what such a wilfully exotic substance might feel like beneath her own nervous fingertips. She remembered the doll herself, and the almost edible pallor of its delicate egg-shaped face.

'How do they do it,' demanded Dierdre, 'grind them?'

'What, the oyster shells?'

'Yes, I wonder.'

Joan was suddenly transported over the years to childhood. She held a paper bag full of mussel shells, and with the little girl next door was busily rubbing them up against the rough bricks of a nearby backyard wall.

'We used to make necklaces,' said present-day Joan excitedly, 'we used to make holes in mussel shells, and thread them on a string, pretend you were a native, from the South Seas, wearing a shell necklace.'

Dierdre looked shifty. 'That must've been nice.' She picked up her big black handbag and swung it rather hard onto the table. 'Time we should be off, I think. If,' she added politely, 'you're finished.'

Joan quickly tilted her cup, and wondered what had happened to the mussel-shell necklaces, and also what could have become of all the little pyramids of soft mussel-shell dust which had fallen as the children rubbed. Mixed long ago, of course with all the multitudinous dusts of London, trodden and scattered beneath a thousand thousand feet.

'Who's with your mother this pee em?' inquired Dierdre as they settled themselves back into the car.

'Who's with – oh, Cissie. She had a day off.'

'Oh yes?' Dierdre squinted busily in all directions as she edged out into the traffic. 'When's her girl getting married?'

'Two weeks, the Saturday it is.'

'Oh yes. Marion, isn't it?'

'Yes. That's her.'

'Saw one of your nephews the other day,' Dierdre added as they pulled up at some traffic lights. Joan listened anxiously to the pleasant tick-tock of the indicator and hoped that Dierdre would soon shut up.

'With ever such a pretty girl. Your other sister Jessie's boy, I think it was. Gareth, his name, isn't it? On a bus. The two of them,' went on Dierdre heavily.

'Oh really?' Joan always felt threatened when Dierdre attempted to discuss the family, as if Dierdre might somehow, in her big groping way, be trying to take them over and introduce herself into the thick of things, when she should know that her place was clearly on the outside.

'Is he engaged as well?' asked Dierdre casually. 'All these weddings you keep going to.'

'Not as far as I know,' replied Joan, also casual. 'We don't see that much of him,' she added, and immediately wished it unsaid.

'And him only living up the road!' marvelled Dierdre. 'Fancy that now. Though of course,' she went on, feeling her way, 'he's a very busy young chap I suppose.' She risked a quick look sideways to see if anything more was forthcoming. Joan's face was averted. Clearly nothing was. Still, it was another toehold. Next time she saw Cissie or Lily she could mention this Gareth slightly disparagingly, as a young man too proud to visit his less elevated relatives might well deserve to be mentioned. And see what happened.

'Same time next week, then?' Dierdre asked finally, as she pulled up beside Joan's door.

'Yes, I should think so. It depends. You know, on someone being in to see to Mum.'

'I'll be in touch.'

Dierdre breathed in masterfully through her nose while Joan made her usual ineffective dabs at the car door.

'Harder! Honestly –' Dierdre leant across and smartly pulled the door to herself. Joan waved her hand; Dierdre raised a brief palm, the signal she also used to acknowledge other motorists who minded their highway manners, and drove away efficiently to her quiet flat in Bow.

Joan, fumbling in her bag for her key, wondered disquietedly about her nephew Gareth, who had done so well, and whether he would ever bestir himself to drop by for a visit, what with him only living up the road, as Dierdre had claimed. Joan had seen Gareth only once since he had left school. He had been frighteningly self-assured even in short trousers, she remembered.

Should she use the best china if he visited, and would it need a wash first after all this time in the cabinet, left to itself? Would he eat ordinary cakes and biscuits for his tea, or would he scorn them as unhealthy? Roughage, that was what modern young doctors all went in for these days, Dierdre had once told her. Would Gareth lecture her about roughage?

I don't care what he says, thought Joan indignantly, pulling off her coat. He'll have to take us as he finds us, inviting himself round here just as he pleases.

And, having succeeded in working up a mood that no one else living could ever divine the cause of, Joan stalked into the kitchen, where Cissie and Lily would be sure to meet one another's eyes as she banged the kettle onto the hob.

Inviting himself here, indeed . . .

THREE

'WHAT's this then, a present?' asked Elizabeth, with that light, glancing irony which sometimes made Gareth wonder if it was time to find someone new.

'Washing,' he said briefly. To escape her eyes he dropped onto his knees and poked his head under the bed, where he remembered seeing a lone sock curled amidst the dust some weeks before. The sea of fluff seemed to have deepened since then, its tides encroaching over a couple of shoeboxes and a spiralled block of filepaper which held someone else's lecture notes, borrowed long since. Gareth scrabbled with his hands and gathered up two fistfuls of hairy fluff. It felt like gritty candy floss. He backed and straightened.

'Where does all this bloody stuff come from?' he demanded, mock-belligerent. His jeans were very tight when he bent over; his face glowed with congestion.

Elizabeth looked down at him with distaste, and imagined herself telling her closest girlfriend, who was unattached and suffering for it, that Gareth's little moods were getting quite tiresome. 'I might just pack him in,' she would add thoughtfully, as one who makes such decisions without fear or risk of future loneliness, 'he's just getting too tedious.'

Aloud she said, 'Why don't you do your own washing, anyway?'

Gareth shaped his two handfuls of fluff into a little rounded heap, discarded it, and burrowed under his bed again. His voice, hooded by bedclothes, was muffled.

'She likes doing it. Makes her feel needed.'

Elizabeth considered this from a feminist viewpoint.

'You don't think much of your mother, do you?' she asked coldly after a pause.

'Got you,' muttered Gareth from beneath the bed. He shuffled backwards, Grey fur clung to his eyebrows and wreathed his stubbled chin. He shook himself comically, but Elizabeth did not smile.

All right then, thought Gareth. All right then! It was a call to self-defence, even to counter-attack. Hadn't he spent all evening trying to smooth over her bad temper, and hadn't she rebuffed his every move?

'She likes fussing over me,' Gareth said, 'she enjoys it.' Elizabeth, he knew, prided herself on her acuity where human needs were involved, liked to think she sighted with ease all the commoner outposts of motivation. 'And I'm her only kid,' Gareth added gently. There, that would blast her. In case it didn't, he decided on a further surprise attack, from the rear this time:

'Anyway, who does *your* washing?'

Beneath this barrage Elizabeth could only retreat.

'I do some of it,' she said distantly. She picked up a lock of her long brown hair and began examining it minutely, looking for split ends. She bit them off when she found them; it was a habit of hers.

Gareth thought briefly of telling her that she looked like a grooming monkey doing that, for God's sake, but decided that this might spark off a larger row than he felt he could handle at present, so instead he asked softly, 'Coming for a drink?'

Elizabeth was silent for a moment. She had been

unpleasant all evening. She had done nothing but criticize him from the moment she had arrived. And still, and still, she reflected bitterly, and still he had not asked her what was wrong. As soon as her tone had sharpened he should have looked into her eyes and asked her why she was so upset. Instead he had taken her mood personally, become defensive, even angry. How could he be so obtuse? It was enough to make her really angry with him in return. But to explain why she was so upset, now, without being asked, seemed out of the question. The only option, really, was to go on being angry with him.

'Maybe I'll just go home,' she said finally, but the mental reiteration of her woes had told on her: her voice quavered with such evident tearfulness that Gareth immediately sat down beside her on the sofa, looked into her eyes, and tenderly asked her what was wrong.

Briefly Elizabeth struggled with herself. She had not intended to make use of tears. Such manoeuvrings were comfort to the enemy, to the conservatives, the women's-place-is-really-in-the-homers. But I'm not crying on purpose, thought Elizabeth with an inner wail, and that makes a difference, doesn't it? Doesn't it? In her heart she knew it did not.

'Come on,' murmured Gareth, his arm cosily about her, 'you can tell me, hmm? Hmm?'

Elizabeth snivelled and capitulated.

'I got the bill for the car, and it's two hundred and forty-two pounds, and I tried to get three intravenous lines in and they all went wrong, all of them, and then I did a history on an old woman, and she had everything wrong with her, I mean, whenever I asked, "Have you had this, or that?" she said, "Oh yes, yes." Only I forgot some, she said, "What about me rheumatoid arthritis, you forgot that one didn't you," and then I took the history sheet to the House Officer and she –'

Elizabeth choked on her tears.

'Yes?'

'And she said, "Is she allergic to anything?" And I'd forgotten to ask.' Elizabeth leaned so heavily upon the last three words that Gareth, recognizing a cue, began,

'Well, everyone forgets that one. Especially at first. I know I forgot to –'

Elizabeth broke in, 'But she, the House Officer! She sort of looked up at the ceiling and, you know, heaved a great sigh. As if, me forgetting, it was just the last straw.'

'What a bag.'

'No, no,' cried Elizabeth eagerly, 'she looked really tired, she had these huge circles under her eyes. Anyway.' Elizabeth wiped her cheeks with the backs of her hands. 'She went off to see the old lady and she came back and she looked at me –'

Gareth surreptitiously looked at his watch. Only an hour to closing time.

'– and I'd just been praying, Oh, don't be allergic to anything, oh, don't be, because you know it had been such an awful day already.'

'And was she?'

'She came back, the House Officer, and she looked at me, and she said, "Well, well, well, better cross this lot out." Because she'd written out the prescriptions, you see. For the old lady. And she had to cross it all out and start again, because the old *crone* was allergic to penicillin, had respiratory arrests on it, the works!'

'You're taking it much too hard,' said Gareth judiciously at this climax. 'Nothing really went wrong, did it? And you'll never forget allergies again, will you, or even rheumatoid?' He smiled coaxingly. 'You know, Medicine,' he finished, quoting a lecturer whom he had forgotten Elizabeth also might have heard, 'is a constant series of narrow escapes.'

Elizabeth made a small smile. Telling Gareth about the miseries of her day had eased their pain, as she had imagined it would. But her evening resentment had not waned. She had played the feminine part all right, she told herself grimly, and he made me do it, he somehow manoeuvred me into it. Or, unhappy thought, had she merely credited Gareth with more intuition than he really possessed? Perhaps no one really had so much?

No, she told herself angrily, catching herself about to shoulder blame, as Woman will whenever she can. No. I wasn't being unreasonable. Men should try harder. Gareth should try harder.

Later in the pub that evening, however, she became quite merry on a pint or two, and said half-jokingly to Gareth.

'I've been brought up to be a woman, you see, that's why I'm the bloody mess I am today!'

Gareth only kissed her, as he'd had a pint or two himself, and told her sentimentally that he loved her just the way she was.

FOUR

LOOKING through the picture window at the back of her lounge Cissie could see her husband Jeff standing, back towards her, hands in his trouser pockets, in the middle of the lawn. Mooning about, she thought, irritated. The irritation, minor enough in itself, gave way suddenly to a great plummeting surge of panic, rather as if she were standing in a fast descending lift, the sort that seems to leave one's stomach behind on a higher floor.

Today was the day. Mother of the bride.

For safety Cissie held onto the edge of the table, and noticed as she did so that Jeff had put the wrong crockery out.

She looked up quickly. There he stood, with his dark narrow head and his big pink ears, and his hands, as usual, in his pockets. Cissie rapped her knuckles on the window, her eyes narrowed. Fiercely she breathed, 'Here!'

Jeff turned at last and saw her but it seemed wonderingly, as if by accident. He jerked his head back in greeting. 'Gormless!' breathed Cissie against the glass. 'Come here,' she mouthed, half pronouncing the words aloud and at the same time beckoning with one meaty arm. Cissie had beaten many a cake and pudding into submission in her time.

Outside Jeff stood in his dew-wet slippers, his legs as heavy as a deep-sea diver's. The day had arrived, despite his mad, shameful hopes. Nothing that could have happened had happened. She had not broken down in tears over some newly arrived set of matching towels, and confessed that it was all over. She had not developed cold feet or pre-wedding nerves of the sort described in Cissie's weekly magazine. Nor had her intended misbehaved; hadn't got drunk, or – perish the thought – bashed her one, or turned out to be married to someone else already.

It was all going to go smoothly, without a hitch, and there was nothing Jeff could do about it. He turned round sadly, resignedly, to go back to the house, and suddenly noticed Cissie waving her fist at him through the window, her lips folded in and her hair all tightly up in curlers, so that her scalp showed through tartan-fashion in little pink squares.

On the warpath all right, he thought glumly, and headed slowly down the crazy-paving and in through the kitchen door.

'What was you thinking of, this is the kitchen stuff, I meant the good china, they'll think this is all I got –'

Jeff sat down at the kitchen table and laid his head down on his folded arms.

'Jeff?'

Cissie looked down at him expressionlessly, but with a familiar twitch of jealousy. When Marion told him she was engaged, the tears had sprung to his eyes; when she said the date was fixed, he had taken to his bed and stayed there for nearly a week, hardly speaking the whole while.

Still, Cissie had lately discovered an explanation for her husband's peculiarities: sitting at the hairdresser's one day, avidly flipping through the old magazines, she had come across an article about modern trends in hospital obstetrics. A man who has seen his baby born, she had read, is simply bound to feel more involved with it than one who has merely paced the floor outside the labour room or got drunk with his mates. It was only natural. Jeff was only natural. Well, thank Christ for that, Cissie had said aloud into the roar of the hairdryer.

And it's different for a man, she had reflected since. How many times had she recounted the story of Marion's birth? The slight backache all day, the faint queasiness attributed to a suspect veal-ham-and-egg pie the night before, the sudden smack and pull of the baby's descent, her own unprecedented view of the underneath of the kitchen table, and Jeff's dinner-plate eyes. How many times had she told the story, breathless with laughter, over the intervening twenty years?

That was how you rid yourself of terrors, by belittling them with laughter. All the same Cissie had often felt uneasy afterwards, almost humiliated, resenting the laughter she had invoked. It was bitter laughter perhaps, because of all that wasted dread, all that fright endured for nothing.

Still, laughing bitterly at your disasters was better than living with them, Cissie thought, staring down at Jeff's bent head. She was sure he had never chatted to anyone about Marion's birth. Not he. Not any man, probably. Not the sort of men I know, anyway, thought Cissie. Men don't talk about anything important. They don't have friends, not really, just their wives' friends' husbands, and their relations and in-laws, and then they only talk about football, or trade unionism, or do-it-yourself, or any bloody thing that's not personal and heartfelt. Poor lonely buggers, that's men, thought Cissie tenderly. She laid a hand on Jeff's shoulder.

'You all right?'

'Yeah. Got to get a shave.' Jeff rose.

'Sure you're all right?'

'Yeah, yeah. Sorry about the cups.'

'Don't you worry about that,' said Cissie indignantly, 'I'll sort that out. You go on up, Marion'll be back soon and she'll want the bathroom God knows how long.'

'Get me glad rags on,' said Jeff with a dreadful smile.

Cissie gave him a kiss.

In the bathroom he looked into his own old face and felt so overwhelmed with purest misery that his eyes filled and ached with tears. Not losing a daughter, but gaining a son. Just let anyone say that to me, he thought to himself, and anger dried his eyes. Just let them try.

For an instant he saw himself, dressed in his best blue, carnation in place, letting his brother-in-law have it right in the eye. Don't want another bleeding son! Wham, right in his little gingery eye.

The wife's relations, that was another dark thought. Hordes of them standing around stuffing themselves at his expense, all taking photographs of one another taking photographs. I could spit, Jeff grimly told his own wan reflection. Spit.

He lathered up. Photographs were all Marion ever talked about lately. As if the photographs were the most important part.

The bridesmaids have to have long dresses, Dad, so they'll look right for the photographs. The bouquet's got to have brown in it, sort of tawny, it's for the photographs. I hope it's a sunny day for the photographs.

Why can't memories be your own private property anymore? wondered Jeff, scraping moodily at his stubble. Private property, that's what memories should be. And what d'you get instead? He eyed his reflection rhetorically. Photographs, that's what. Little fixed rectangles, unchangeable, never blurring pleasantly with time, never quite out of the reach of strangers.

Photographs. The way she talked, you'd think it was all she was doing it for. A fat white album for her coffee table, to show to her friends.

He imagined her small round face over the album, pointing out relatives to new friends, pointing out himself.

'And that's my dad.'

Jeff put down his razor, for his eyes had overflowed.

Downstairs Marion let herself in and went to the kitchen to find her mother.

'Well?' She stood upright and slowly turned herself round. 'What d'you think of it?'

'*Very* nice,' said Cissie immediately. She reached out a hand to the stiff crown of curls, but Marion jerked herself away.

'Don't touch it!'

'Makes you look older,' said Cissie weepily.

'Oh, can it,' said Marion mildly. She looked in the mirror by the backdoor. Was it right, really, the hairdo? It didn't quite look as she had imagined it would, but in what way was it different? And did it make her face look fatter? She sucked her cheeks in. That was where you put the blusher. She had read about it in so many articles: How to Find Your Cheekbones.

'See these?' Marion waggled her stubby hands at her mother. The girl in the hairdresser's had glued long plastic fingernails over Marion's own chewed ones, and lacquered them a brilliant glossy scarlet. 'Look at that!'

'My God,' said Cissie, in wonder and alarm. Was that how the film stars did it? 'How are you going to get your make-up on?'

'Oh, all right,' shrugged Marion vaguely. I hadn't thought of that. Trust your mum to think of something like that.

'Wool, you'd best hurry up, I'm dishing up soon.'

The thought of hurrying with these bloody nails on made Marion panic. She scuttled up the stairs, as once long before she had scuttled up them screeching, with one of her brothers roaring after her, because she had sat on his balsa-wood aeroplane.

On the landing she met her father in his vest, his face all over clots and bits of pale green toilet paper.

'God almighty, Dad, you got the shakes?'

'Looks very nice,' said Jeff feebly, smiling at her hair. He supposed it was right to have your hair done up for your wedding. But it looked very tight somehow. 'Very smart.'

'You finished in the bathroom?'

'Oh. Yes. All yours.'

'Wool. See you downstairs then, all right, Dad?'

'Right.'

And she had got past him and gathered up the bagsful of stuff she needed, and was in the bathroom and bolting the door behind her before he could say anything more. What would he have said, had she lingered? Anything at all?

Downstairs the doorbell gave out its jaunty chimes. They'd begun to arrive, then, that coy, joking, done-up-like-dogs'-dinners horde of bloody in-laws.

Gaining a son, eh? Just let them try.

FIVE

IT came to Gareth, as he sat beside his mother on Marion's side of the church, that he really enjoyed his relatives these days. Somehow over the last few years he had acquired a taste for them, a pleasure in their company unimaginable in the days of his adolescence, when he had been extravagantly ashamed of them. How carefully, when questioned, he had once spoken of London, never Stepney or Hackney or Bethnal Green! How on occasion he had sweated at night, imagining the living connections between himself and these unutterably lower-caste places all discovered, and himself thus shorn of all credit in the power-games of friendship!

It was amusing to look back on, that period of uncomplicated snobbery. He had been so unselfconscious about his hatred; could with a cheerful heart have struck dead every aunt and uncle, every soul of his kith and kin down to the smallest cousin-in-arms, to prevent the secret of their existence from falling into the hands of Edwards, or of Lloyd-Jones, or of any other of the Greater Powers of Form IIa.

His later tactics, as his twenties neared, had been less honest. The memory of them made Gareth uncomfortable, made the pew hard. He shifted himself sideways and crossed his legs. He seemed to remember hauling his mother's family into every political and sociological argument he had been involved in, and he had been involved in at least one a day, or had there simply been one continuous term-long argument, crackling away like a little bonfire in the common room, its flames fed every lunch hour by whoever passed by?

'Take my aunt Joan for instance. A victim of the system. Won a scholarship place at a good school, and couldn't take it, because her mother couldn't afford the uniform . . .

'Oh yes, good point, good point. Why don't you go and explain it all to my uncle Jim, who's got two jobs and a disability pension and lives in a basement flat in Stepney? He'd love to buy a council house, you just tell him how he can do it and still afford luxuries like, you know, food and that –'

He had used them not only against his enemies, but to gain power amongst his friends. His own politics, Gareth had implied over that sixth-form bonfire, had been formed from personal involvement, from class injustices plain before his eyes, from the Word made his very own flesh-and-blood; whereas his schoolfellows were acting on merely intellectual convictions, suspiciously fashionable at the time and anyway not nearly so romantic.

In his last year at school Gareth had cautiously begun to imitate the English of his mother's family, lightly to drop an aitch here and there, to soften a g-sound somewhere else, particularly when angered, as he had read many novels in which characters dropped their assumed voices in times of crisis. It seemed now to Gareth's pyrexial memory that he had announced his intention to enter Medicine in tones strongly reminiscent of the Artful Dodger.

Gareth twitched his shoulders under his good suit jacket and uttered a little groan of denial, which he turned easily into a convincing congregational cough. Was being aware now of all these past machinations, being wryly aware of them, enough to cancel them out?

Gareth told himself that it was. That if he were properly conniving and dishonest, past connivings and dishonesties would not now rise and reproach him. All this embarrassment was his apology, both to his sixth-form colleagues and to his mother's abused family. And whatever he had once felt about his relatives, he liked them well enough now. Accepted them. He remembered Oscar Wilde on parents: that one begins by loving them, later judges, and ends, sometimes, by forgiving them.

Evidently he had forgiven this lot, he thought, glancing around him. He felt positively happy in their presence here gathered together. Now why was this? Not simply through nostalgia for the faces he had known since babyhood. No, it was something more. Was it, perhaps, that he had left them all behind? No need now to secrete or exploit them; no need, in fact, to do anything about them ever again. They were left far behind, the whole motley pantomime bunch of them, fat overbearing aunts and dreary unionizing uncles and all their hapless hopeless progeny. All far behind, and all thus forgiven.

Somewhere to Gareth's right, organ music began to bubble and pop with featureless melody. Gareth heard it with nostalgia. It sounded exactly like the parish church organ of his childhood: the same bland popping treble line, the same uncomfortable impression of mechanical strain about the bass. Church music: music to keep still to, music to be sat through.

The sound of it reminded him abruptly of other more fraught childhood Sundays spent visiting his grandmother and that slight, smoky shade her husband. They were booked well in advance, those visits, like diplomatic tours by heads of state. By virtue of distance, living out in Kent as she did, and by certain small differences in matters of household management and child-rearing, Jessie had

43

established herself as a separate branch of the family, an independent state, a colony reluctantly but officially granted full independence and self-rule, quite distinct from the humming neighbourly satellite Cissie or the entirely sub-jugated territories represented by Aunt Joan.

The visitors' reception would therefore be gracious or chilly. Lily would embrace her daughter with restraint, as if recalling the good old days of Jessie's childhood and the gun-boat diplomacy of a smart cuff round the ear. Gareth himself, that second-generation Kentish foreigner, she teased and petted by turns; he made her feel uncomfortable.

As Lily released her daughter, Lily's husband, that small sandy shadow at Lily's shoulder, would slide forward, his left hand cupped protectively about his glowing roll-up.

''Lo kid. 'Lo Jess. 'Lo Jess darlin'.' He would then touch his stubbly cheek briefly against Jessie's smooth one, push Gareth very gently on one shoulder, and retreat back to the kitchen fireside and the evening paper, which he would hold firmly before his eyes no matter what sounds of imminent battle reached his ears. Sometimes he turned a page.

Early male role-model, thought Gareth in the church, remembering the calm rustle of newspaper over the fierce Cold-War summitry next door. Not Man the Hunter or Man the Aggressor. No, not Grandad. More like Man the Bored Onlooker, Man the Imperturbable Audience of Cosmic Differentials.

And each visit's dreadful climax: the tea all laid out in the cold front room; always a salad with pink tinned salmon and balefully dripping beetroot and one of Aunt Joan's sinister sponge-cakes looming on the sideboard. They were squat and yellow, those sponge-cakes, volcanic, their cracked and pointed apices faintly threatening eruption.

The organ music swelled suddenly, as if somewhere something were reaching boiling point. Gareth remem-bered the feel of the half-crown, hot and lightly greasy, that Lily had pressed into his hand at the visit's end, over Jessie's ritual protests and his own schooled murmurings, 'Oh, no thank you Granny, I couldn't possibly.' Joyous with relief they would begin the long trip home and on the way Jessie would re-tell one of her stories about Lily, as if to counteract any favourable impression left by the half-crown:

'Wool I finished that dress, it was the first thing I'd ever made, and I'd saved up so long for the material, and spent ages doing it just right, French sewing on the seams and finishing it all off. Then I tried it on. And it didn't fit, didn't fit anywhere! Miles too small! Because I'd forgotten to leave anything for the seams. And when I told Mum, I was in tears, she just laughed and laughed, and d'you know what she said?'

A small pause for Gareth, who knew exactly what Lily had said, to shake his head expectantly.

'I'll tell you what she said. She said, "I saw what you was doing, straight off. Coulda told you weeks ago, you silly little cow," she said to me. And she laughed, she nearly cried laughing. And maybe it wasn't true, what she said. Maybe she hadn't known, she was just making it up. It was the sort of thing she'd do, see.'

There she sat, two pews ahead, beneath a white old-ladyfied hat. Who was that beside her under a wide-brimmed acid green? Gareth stared hard, and presently the brim rotated, and in its jaundiced shade he caught Aunt Joan's big excitable smile. As she turned back he had a mental picture, so vivid that he was convinced of its truth, of Lily telling Joan that the colour suited her, and brought out the colour of her eyes. Poor old batty Joan. Clearly she had never worked through any normal adolescent reaction phase against her mother, remaining child-dependent all her days. Gareth sat up straight in the pew, suddenly alert to his own thoughts: you might begin by loving, judging, and forgiving your relatives, but nowadays you went on to *diagnose* them. Gareth smiled. It was good. Sometimes you forgive them, then you diagnose them. It would impress.

Definitely. But how to introduce it? Impossible, unless someone else quoted the appropriate bit of Wilde, or the effect would be too heavy, self-advertising. I'll simply have to wait for a graceful opportunity, Gareth decided. It may take years. It might, he realized, take so long that by the time someone said the right opening line, he would have forgotten the cap to it, be left stammering over some distant future dinner-table, 'Ooh, ah, wait a minute, ooh, what was it now,' and clicking his fingers.

He was awoken from this frustrating fantasy by the sudden urgent wail of the Bridal March. Hats bobbed and revolved, order sheets fluttered. The churchful of forgiven relatives rose noisily to its feet. The March boomed; Marion and Uncle Jeff passed into Gareth's line of vision. She was at least an inch taller than Jeff, Gareth saw, and what huge shoulders she had! Rather like an American football player in her daisy-spotted veil; he glanced down at Jessie, who moved her dark eyebrows slightly in return. Gareth peered forward. There was Marion's intended, looking engagingly nondescript.

No one in this whole church to touch Me, thought Gareth, and he allowed himself a few moments of tingling euphoria, but only a few, in case the Fates should eavesdrop on his happiness and step in to put things right; and he sang very loudly at the first hymn, just to confuse them.

Outside the church afterwards the crowd whooped and chattered and bunched together with something of the glad exhilaration of survival. A light rain had fallen and the air smelt cleanly of damp city dust. Beyond the gates cars and lorries whisked by as if this were an ordinary day.

Beside the church the cameras had begun to roll.

'Now you and Jim.'

'Where's Sharon? She in this one?'

'Smile, Dad!'

'Say cheese!'

That's all it was for, the whole bloody performance, thought Jeff as he smiled, Cissie on his arm resplendent in her rippling peacocks: for photographs. Just for the photographs. For a set of coherent images, readily dateable.

'Now you and the bride, please.'

For the latest bulwark against mortality, as if the present can be made to keep by preserving images of it, as a batch of soft fruit can be made to keep by bottling it with sugar.

'And Mum too.'

Attuned by grief Jeff saw with clarity the connection between the immortal image and the ephemeral self; saw it, inspected it, and said to himself, 'I hate bloody wedding photographs.'

'Ay-ar, mate! Father of the bride. How's it feel then, eh?' Jeff held out his hand. It was Jimmy, the brother-in-law whose eye he had dreamt of blacking, plump gingery Jim.

'Nice to see you, Jim.'

'One more off of your hands, eh, one more out of the old nest.'

Was he going to say it?

'Very lucky lad, young Barry.'

He was.

'But still, eh? Gaining a son, eh?'

Instead of the wave of aggression Jeff had anticipated, the sound of these words flooded him with a sudden enervating rush of sympathy, for suffering deluded mankind in general and thick-headed gingery Jim in particular, so that fresh tears warmed his eyes and Jim, emboldened by the evident success of his remarks, remembered his professional position and moved in for the kill.

'Here,' he said, flicking Jeff rather hard on the chest with his pale freckled fingers. 'Here. Are they in on our Young Marrieds Scheme?'

47

Lily sat on the chair someone had brought her from the vestry and watched the throng without interest. Her teeth, glued to her unaccustomed jaws, felt grossly outsized, like a set of dentures designed for a mastiff. These modern weddings, she thought, were all the same: a church, a meal, a speech, and Bob's-your-uncle. No real music, no dancing, no drinking, no excitement. No fun.

Lily remembered the wedding of her old friend Maggsie just after the Great War, when the wedding party had lasted all the wedding-night long, and the bride, her determination to begin as she meant to go on fortified by a great deal of gin, had laid out cold her drunken bear of a brother-in-law, by swinging round her head and at his a net shopping bag containing six tins of sardines-in-tomato-sauce, snatched from a passing shopper for the purpose.

One of her best stories once; not in fashion now. Like the wedding of Lily's own sister Phyllis, which had developed into a memorable party, brought to a close only when the groom's aged grandmother, her sense of balance undermined by her years, had slipped backwards off the trestle table where she had been shrilly cackling and doing a knees-up, and broken a leg on the linoleum floor below.

Weddings these days weren't for fun at all, thought Lily, but meant to show how posh you were. The little glass of wine over the breakfast, the salad full of nasty foreign new-fangled bits-and-bobs, and the solitary glass of champagne to toast the happy couple with at the end. They were all part and parcel, Lily thought, of this same tiresome aping of the gentry which always somehow involved stamping all the fun out of things.

No beer, no stout,

thought Lily, to the tune of 'Nowell'.

No ale, sold out,
Born is the king with his
Tongue hanging out.

48

'Smile, Mum! Here's Marion, stand behind her Marion, that's right, where's Barry, Barry! Over here, no, over there, move your bouquet a bit will you, no the other way, now, cheese!'

It was gentility that had infected her children and her grandchildren, Lily thought. They were all too busy being toffs to have a good time. A wedding, and no beer!

'Smile, Nana!'

Dutifully Lily bared the dentures at the cameras, and the lights flashed and flashed.

'It's a pay-your-own-way situation,' Jimmy went on, 'which the Liaison Committee *has* decided to unequivocably support *for* young people within the confines *of* our Jurisdiction.'

Joan was putting in some serious worrying about her dress. Wouldn't she, after all, have been better off with the blue-grey, getting more wear out of it than with this more unusual shade? 'What an unusual colour!' Jessie had warmly said that morning. 'Very nice! Brings out the colour of your eyes.' And Jessie knew about such things. But, thought Joan, you couldn't wear a colour like this for every day. It would soon spoil. You'd have to keep it for best, for special occasions when eyes particularly needed to be brought out.

But then special occasions didn't come round that often, so would you get your money's worth that way after all? If only you could change the colour or style of things by wishing, see what everyone else was wearing and then, like a chameleon, wish yourself to blend in . . .

'Just you remember this,' whispered Cissie, fierce with emotion, 'if ever you see me getting like her, if ever you see me doing something she'd do, just tell me! You say, "Mum! You're getting just like your mother!" Eh? Will you? Tell me?'

Marion nodded. 'All right.' It was funny, she thought. One of her own fears was getting to be like Cissie. Was every girl in fear of growing up like Mum? Marion frowned. She had made the jump from the personal to the general, and had no idea what to do next.

Well, it was hardly the day to bother with such things now, she felt. Aloud she said, 'Is me veil still straight?'

'Sausages by their very nature need a preservative.'

Gareth gulped helplessly.

Uncle Jim was unperturbed.

'We have been involved in a survey on hams for a period of two years –'

She was going, she was climbing into the car with him. The first separation; short, but still the first of all. Jeff waved with the crowd, flung a forbidden handful of coloured bits of paper shaped into tiny rings and horseshoes.

In his heart he saw a summer night in 1958, and Cissie astonished on the kitchen floor, while a first little triangle of furred skull came peeping between her legs. He saw himself watching, dazed with terror, as the triangle enlarged itself, became recognizably and overwhelmingly the back of someone's head. He had caught the baby as she slithered free, turning like a plump wet fish in his hands.

He had almost forgotten Cissie then, as she lay back, still stunned, against the table-leg. He had looked into the baby's face, and the baby, its eyes alert and shining, had looked back with a stately calm and simplicity.

Ever since then Jeff had felt a hollow man when he was parted from his daughter, as if she had taken something from him; though not greedily, not with malice.

They had gone. She had gone. He was a bereaved man, and not allowed to grieve.

Gone. He waved a hand, losing a daughter.

Gone.

'Hasn't Cissie put on weight!' exclaimed Jessie as they drove through Sidcup. 'She told me she never eats pastry or sweets or ice-cream, I think she does but she's usually so busy talking she doesn't know what she's eating, see –'

Jessie was exhilarated. It was so seldom she saw the family, living out in Kent as she did, and the sight of them all alive and healthy was a wonderful comfort, she thought. She was also deeply aware of the extent of Cissie's jealousy over Gareth's success, a jealousy which, Jessie reminded herself, she, Jessie, had done absolutely nothing to encourage, giving Gareth only the slightest little mention when she and Cissie had had their chat. Whereas, of course, if it had been one of Cissie's own children who had advanced so well, Cissie would never have let anyone forget it, dragging the successful one into any old conversation, you could just bet on it.

But then, of course, thought Jessie, Cissie and I were always so different.

'I don't think Marion's dress helped, exactly, do you?' she asked aloud.

Gareth grinned at the road ahead. 'It was her hair, I think. Pure 1962. I was thinking, I expect it was done by some girl whose life sort of climaxed just then, in 1962, and she's been turning out beehives ever since.'

Jessie giggled and tutted. 'Did you speak to your poor Aunt Joan at all?'

'Oh yes. Chatted at the reception, you know. She wasn't quite with us, I thought.'

'You talk about the Hospital?'

'A bit. I tried. I said, "I expect it's all changed a great deal since then," and she said, Yes, she supposed it had, too. End of conversation.'

'She used to work so hard there, during the War.'

'Mm?' Gareth saw that his mother was enjoying herself. She always talked about the past, he had noticed, when she was particularly happy and excited, as if she had to wait until the present was at its very best before she could risk any comparisons. Could that be true, he wondered, glancing over at her animated face. A function of ageing, perhaps? She was still telling the story of Joan and her brief uncomfortable career; he tuned in:

'Forty pounds a year I think it was, and the night duty! It was like being in the army, but worse maybe, all the holier-than-thouing and you know poor Joan could never stand up for herself anyway, all marching to the wards in single file and not allowed to talk to the doctors, not so much as to say good morning, did you know that? Only the sisters could talk to the doctors.'

Gareth tuned out again. The yellow-lit suburbs had given way to the waving darkness of trees. Not a bad idea at all, he was thinking: Ho, silence on the ward there. Dr Williams is approaching. Pray silence for the Doctor. Not at all a bad idea. He could think of more than a few nurses whose overall behaviour might be wonderfully improved by a little enforced silence. Gareth sighed into the darkness, reconsidering that chafing mystery: his own continuing unpopularity with the nurses.

It simply wasn't fair: he never nagged or criticized them publicly, or made them take fifteen-minute observations unless it was strictly necessary, and he always allowed the night nurses to make him cups of tea. And yet he was not liked. Not disliked, particularly, but not liked; denied that interesting mixture of sexual and professional respect he had sensed was eagerly served up to others. Not that it really mattered, of course, Gareth told himself. Not that it really mattered what they thought, those bitches. And yet –

('You try to flirt with them all at once, that's what's wrong,' Elizabeth had charged one recent rather drunken evening, using her light ironic voice. 'You swagger amongst them; I saw you at it, that time on Patience ward, remember? You went up to the desk and said, "I need a nurse for a ward-round, can I choose the prettiest?" It's humiliating. Of course they don't like it. But one or two of them will smile back, to be polite, because women are always so polite! And maybe because' – Elizabeth had raised her glass to him, sarcastically – 'because you're a bit of a prize after all; and the ones who don't smile back despise the ones who do, and so there's an unpleasant atmosphere amongst them, all traceable to you. As usual: as men always will cause dissension among women.'

'Thought about this a lot, have you?' he had demanded in tones as close to Elizabeth's own as he could manage. He had been annoyed, abashed, and tremendously excited to think that Elizabeth put so much effort into understanding him; though also dismayed to see how completely his little ploy on Patience ward, designed to sharpen her love with a touch of jealousy, had misfired.

'Thought about this a lot, have you?'

'A fair amount. It's pure sex-war, doctors and nurses. 'Cept for the likes of me re-drawing the battle-lines. But there's always an infallible way to be popular with nurses, if you really want to know how. I only wish it was open to me, that's all.'

He had relaxed a little then, realizing that this angry contempt was not really directed at himself. A great many of Elizabeth's fiercer opinions, he had noticed, were obliquely powered by quite unconnected personal bitternesses. As now. It was rather an endearing lack of sophistication on her part, he felt. What had happened to prompt this salvo? Had some ward sister snubbed her, had some student nurse told her to go away during report?

'What way?' he had tenderly inquired.

'You just have to marry one, that's all,' replied Elizabeth coldly. 'Marry a nurse and no matter what sort of sod you are, as you stalk away the nurses will turn to one another and say approvingly, "Oh, he's married to a nurse." Means you don't despise them, you see. How can you, they think, if you're married to one of their own? But that's all wrong of course, isn't it, men prefer to marry women they can despise. Don't they?' Elizabeth had demanded fiercely. 'Don't they?')

Gareth sighed again, at the memory of this unspeakably dreary conclusion, and tuned in to Jessie again.

'But then my mother always did thwart Joan,' Jessie was saying, 'she was the cleverest of us all, you know, the brainiest.'

Here comes the scholarship, thought Gareth gloomily. He remembered the sixth-form bonfire, and briefly suffered a tiny irritant stab of guilt, small and sharp as a splinter in a nail-bed.

'When she was in the top class she won a scholarship to a secondary school, a good school it was in those days, and Mum said No, she couldn't go, because all the other kids'd win it too, and she wouldn't be able to afford the uniforms. That's what she said, and I've never forgiven her for it, I've thought of it often. I mean, Cissie and Jimmy just weren't that way inclined, *and* she knew it. Maybe me, but I was so much younger anything could've happened before I got to that age and it did, too, the War and everything –'

There it was, thought Gareth, the glum ring of Truth. Mother said No. And so farewell independence, farewell maturity, farewell to heaven knew what life might have held. It was a nasty story, a story with parallels. He had been an effortless prize-winner himself. There but for the grace of social change ...

'Did you know,' Gareth said suddenly, happily remembering gossip, 'that Joan's got some suspiciously butch friend, who takes her out once a week?'

'What d'you mean?' asked Jessie sharply. Gareth saw at once that he had gone too far. After all there was a limit, he told himself, to the sexual sophistication a man can expect from his own mother.

'Cissie's eldest, the electrician,' said Gareth lightly, 'he told me they go to Bethnal Green Museum to look at the dolls.'

'You know that Cissie's eldest,' cried Jessie excitedly, 'he got his eleven-plus and he never passed another exam in his life, not one O level did he get, not one, he was working down the grocer's evenings and Saturdays, couldn't do his homework see, poor little tyke. See, Cissie thought grammar school was *it*, see?'

And so, no doubt, did her eldest, Gareth thought. Because that's what class is all about: class lies in the aspirations of one's children.

'Aren't you going just a weeny bit too fast, lovey?'

'Oh ... sorry,' Gareth slowed the car down. Was it me, he was wondering, or did I just remember it? Class lies in the aspirations of one's children. It was jolly good anyway. It was true. Look at me, he thought. Look at Cissie's eldest.

'Cissie had hardly a civil word to say to me,' lamented Jessie as they neared her own front door. 'And,' she added virtuously, 'I don't know what she's got to be so cool about. I haven't done anything.'

'I see her boy come on his own,' scowled Cissie as she wrenched her hair back into curlers for what remained of the night. Her fingers flew: the pale pink squares re-tartaned.

Jeff was silent. He had not undressed. He lay limply on the bed and looked up at the ceiling.

'You know why she never re-married, my sister Jessie?' asked Cissie grimly. 'I'll tell you why. Because she's always had that smarmy son of hers, that's why!'

Jeff swallowed with some difficulty.

Cissie turned back to the mirror and began to dab moisturizer beneath her eyes. She was already regretting that she had uttered just this same speech to Jimmy's Carol at the reception, because Jimmy's Carol was quite likely to pass the tidbit on to Lily, who would undoubtedly take the very first opportunity to pass it on to Jessie herself, with possible embellishments.

Oh, but I'm too tired to worry about all that now, thought Cissie. All over at last, thank God. They'd be in Ibiza by now. Maybe even tucked up in bed already. Cissie looked at her own shining face in the mirror. Poor Marion. Marriage was always a bit of a disappointment, any woman could vouch for that. Still, remembered Cissie, at least the wedding-night won't be too much of a shock for her, and that's a comfort.

Removing the white armchair, which had quickly grown itself a fitted cover of dark green liquid velvet, Joan had decided to branch out: abandoning the single key item, she had settled on a chaise longue with two matching lamp-standards so that the fish could take turns to lounge in a good light. A nice light-oak bookcase would have looked well, too, Joan thought.

'I'll see what I can do,' Joan promised. The goldfish continued their gentle motion, as peaceful as cardboard fish in a mobile.

'Her Jeff's gone bald,' Joan whispered very softly.

The green dress hung safely inside the wardrobe, waiting for its next outing, whenever that might be.

Too bright for a funeral, hissed Joan's own resident Lady Macbeth, but Joan hardly heard.

'Good night, you fish,' she whispered, her fingertips against the glass. The fish remained dumb, so she thought their reply for them:

'Night night, Joan.'

Beside her as she slept the goldfish circled their drowned drawing-room; in the dim light from the lamp-post outside they gleamed and vanished, gleamed and vanished, turning into the darkness, sleepless and confined.

SIX

IT was the evening of the last day of October, and Lily was in bed early, troubled by a new cough. She lay propped up against her pillows, her head tilted back a little, her arms neat and straight upon the eiderdown: Joan, leaving her for the night, had been reminded of the languid miniature mistress of the Gate Baby House in her carpeted four-poster.

'Call me if you need me, now.'

'Yeah, yeah.'

Lily sighed. From downstairs came the familiar sounds of gunfire and screams: Joan at the TV again. From across the street, through several thicknesses of wall and stretches of space, came a faint throb of Reggae bass: *doo* dooby doo dooby *doo* dooby ... The blacks on the corner must be throwing another party, Lily thought. She had often watched them through the front-room curtains, the lanky loose-kneed young men, their hair packed into brightly coloured bag-like woollen hats, the women in plastic flip-flop sandals for the summer, the baby girls with their hair twisted into plaits like tiny twigs.

They made the streets look foreign: they turned the familiar streets of Stepney into a foreign city, as if Place were not an immutable reality fixed by landmarks of brick and concrete, but a mere transient result of human habits, and nearly as changeable as weather.

As if England were not necessarily England at all, or Dunnett Street Dunnett Street, or Number Fifty-One Number Fifty-One, names existing only to clarify the present. And the present might profoundly alter at any moment, when the sounds of an evening's entertainment had collected themselves into native drumbeats: *doo* dooby *doo* dooby *doo* dooby . . .

All this Lily felt as a mild resentment of that newly familiar rhythm, and put occasionally into speeches about Taking Our Jobs, and Putting Up the Crime Rate; but in truth only the challenge to Place distressed her. It compounded the changes, the brick-and-concrete changes, that she had noticed anew during last week's drive to Marion's wedding: the new flats and straining tower-blocks, the waste-ground car-parks, the corrugated iron fences plastered with posters and aerosol paint, all the landmarks of the new foreign city. At the same time, as in a film double-exposed, she had seen the ghostly outlines of earlier streets and houses, the structural ghosts of the old vanished city.

Lived here sixty years, thought Lily, putting her cloudy thoughts suddenly into words, Lived here sixty years and I'd be lost two streets away. Sixty years in one house. Making up for all those earlier years of short lets and lodging-houses. Lily closed her eyes, and behind the lids saw clearly the first-floor back her own mother had rented in Poplar, when the old Queen had still been immortal.

Lily's mother sat by the tall window for the light, and sewed up a tear in her own green worsted jacket. Lily saw the wrinkled empty sleeve of it sag across her mother's lap, the sly gaping wrist of it mouth and eye combined, the baggy creature of half-a-dozen nightmares.

Lily's mother sat by the bed and sang. She sang her own small repertoire of music-hall songs, but very slowly and sadly, transposed into minor keys and defused of all jollity.

> Oh, I wonder what it feels like to be poor,
> To forever have the wolf around your door,

Lily could see her now, her hair all straggled down and her hem-line trailing, singing intently for herself, her eyes closed, her hands folded in her lap:

> Only last week over tea
> Baron Rothschild said to me,
> Oow, I wonder what it feels like
> To be poo-ar!

Lily smiled, her eyes still closed. She was listening to the tragic reproach, the heartbreakingly muted despair of her mother's own particular rendition of

> Who were you with last night,
> Out in the pale moonlight?

Now there was an interesting question, Lily thought, as the soft voice faded. Hard thinking brought her father briefly into focus, a memory snap-shot of a thin shadowed face beneath a peaked cap. There had been a story about him, told by Lily's own mother, and passed on by Lily to her own children, when they were small.

My dad, thought Lily, mentally re-telling the story to these same small children, was a haddock-smoker down Limehouse way. One day his boss says to him, You got to do the crabs today. His other lad hadn't shown, see.

'You do the crabs today,' says the boss to my dad.

'What do I do?' says my dad.

Boss gives him a look. 'Boil 'em,' he says. 'Boil 'em up well.'

So off my dad goes to the crab vat. This was down on the docks, see. There's the vat. Looks in. Sees all these crabs, all climbing about, alive-alive-o, see? Off he goes back to the boss.

'Here, them crabs. They're still alive!'

Boss says, 'So boil 'em up, that'll do for 'em!'

My dad, he can't believe it.

'What, boil 'em up alive,' he says, 'boil 'em up alive?'

Boss gets mad. 'That's right,' he shouts, 'and you bloody get a move on!'

'Can't do that,' says my dad. 'Can't do it.'

'I'll find someone what can then,' says the boss straight back.

'You do that,' says my dad, and he pulls his hat down, and he runs off back to the vat, picks it up, arms right round it – it's got water in it too – and staggers off with it, and the crabs all swinging up and down, and splosh turns it over the side into the Thames, all them crabs over the side into the water and off.

Lily in her bed studied her picture of him then, his boots skidding over the wet cobbles, a crowd about him cheering for recklessness, the fishmonger dancing with rage. A shame she had been forced to invent so much of the story herself: a shame her father, dismissed, had simply put his wet fishy hands back in his pockets and mooched off home.

> Who were you with last night,
> Out in the pale moonlight?
> It wasn't your sister,
> It wasn't your ma,

How old was she, Lily wondered, when she died? I was fifteen, so she couldn't have been more than thirty-five; younger than all my kids are now. I left her on the sofa, I ran upstairs to the neighbours: Mrs Knapper.

'My mum's ill, she's dying!'

Mrs Knapper was sitting at the table, eating something out of a teacup with a spoon. She set the cup down carefully before she got up but she hung onto the spoon. It stuck out of her big fist as she hammered down the stairs, holding up a bunch of her skirt in the other hand.

Lily's mother lay as Lily left her, without a mark on her.

Mrs Knapper knelt down by the settee and laid two fingers on her neighbour's bosom, where she thought the heart might be.

'Got a mirror?'

Lily unhooked the small spotted mirror over the washstand, very carefully, as she didn't want seven years' bad luck on top of everything else.

'She's gone, I reckon,' said Mrs Knapper. She took the mirror and held it against the white lips.

'Nothing, see?' She pointed with the spoon still held in her other hand. 'No mist. She's passed away. You got to get a doctor. Did you send?'

'No. I just come upstairs.'

'You go off now then. Get Cohen, he's cheapest, sorry about that in front of her but there it is, I'll sit with her.'

Lily hesitated. If she left now, went out through the door, her mother would really be very dead by the time she returned, whereas if she stayed her mother might remain only just dead, just dead this instant, for a little while longer, as if there was still some transition to be got through, as if death were not, yet, quite final.

'What are you waiting for?' asked Mrs Knapper. She put the spoon down on the mantelpiece and pulled up a stool to sit beside the settee.

Outside the March air had been bright and blowy. Lily had walked quickly, then faster and faster, until she had finally begun to run. Over at last, the death that filled all horizons. On my own, Lily's heart had sung as she sped through the windy streets, on my own now, and everything all before me.

Forgot my own sister, thought old Lily, faintly grinning in her bed. Forgot poor little Phyllis. Well, everyone always had. A lot like daft Joanie, was Phyllis. Nine when mother died. Who had put her in the convent school, who was responsible for that? Can't remember now, thought Lily. She was growing drowsy. The native drumbeats had silenced, and her feet at last were warming.

When I went to meet Phyllis leaving the convent, she was afraid to get in the bus. A motorbus, that's all it was.

'What's this instrument of the devil?' she screeches. I just hauled her on, all pop-eyed and screaming, people must've thought she was touched.

'What's this instrument of the devil?'

For a giddy moment, Lily swung out over the moving pavement, one hand clamped around the passenger rail, the other fast in Phyllis's coat-collar.

'No!' squealed Phyllis, running dementedly along beside the bus, 'No, no, no, no!' and she leapt onto the running-board beside Lily and clutched at her, wild-eyed, while Lily whooped with laughter.

'Come on, let's sit down, for God's sake!'

The bus was quite empty inside. Lily noticed a certain strange darkness at the bright edges of things, as if all she saw were framed with night.

'Why are you lying down?' asked Phyllis. Lily was embarrassed. Perhaps the bus had started too quickly. She could remember falling now, and the hard smack of the wooden floor upon her hip and shoulder. She wondered if she should try to get up, but there seemed no real reason why she should. She was quite comfortable stretched out in the aisle. No one seemed to want to step past her. It was a very quiet bus.

'Told you there was nothing to get scared about,' she remarked to Phyllis.

Phyllis had changed. She had bobbed her hair and put black stuff round her eyes.

'Meeting a chap tonight,' she said, smirking. She crossed her legs. 'Got a fag?'

Lily felt carpet beneath her fingers, and remembered that

Phyllis had been run over in 1936, and killed, though not by a bus. Lily was perplexed.

'I thought you were alive, Phyll!'

'Bin dead for years!' cried Phyllis, her black-rimmed eyes gleaming, and she laughed so long and hard that her face seemed all gaping cavernous mouth and eye combined, and her body stretched and dwindled into something baggy and greenish, that tip-toed ever closer on its own brass buttons, still hooting with snaky laughter.

Lily struggled, screamed, unable to run for the wriggling parcels she held in her arms, and all the while the bus roared faster and faster, further and further away from the city lights and the streets of home.

'Oh, help me, Jesus!'

Lily awoke. For a moment she experienced absence, lying still without any thought or feeling at all. Then she remembered that she had been dreaming again, and of something too horrible to bear, too horrible to look fully upon. She would not think about it: she would forget it utterly.

'Just a dream,' Lily said aloud, to hurry the unprobed mass of nightmare more quickly into oblivion, 'just a dream.' As she spoke she noticed that her face felt strange, that speech felt wrong. She moved her lips again, experimentally, and discovered that she was lying on the floor beside the bed, her cheek pressed firmly to the bedside rug.

Lily moved her head slightly, and sniffed the dust. Fallen out of bed, she thought comfortably, and without surprise; poor old sod's fallen out of bed. She moved her eyes to look about her. Everything looked so different from this dust's-eye-view. The bedside table loomed as steeply as a new London skyscraper, the chest of drawers bulged like an Edwardian matron, juttingly rotund.

It was very quiet, and quite dark but for the yellow line of light beneath the door. Lily lay still, looking at that yellow strip for some time, until at last over the mild, confused calm of her thoughts a small interference began, like a foreign radio on a crowded wavelength. First a mere crackling, then a hum of speech, and finally a rude chattering counterpoint pushed aside all content and announced clearly:

I am an old woman and I have taken a fall and hurt myself, and how much longer must I lie here injured in the dark and all alone?

Lily summoned as much of her old force, as much of her real self, as she could, raised her head, and bellowed indignantly for her daughter Joan.

SEVEN

BEFORE risking it with a more general public, Gareth had decided to try out his snippet of Wildean repartee on Elizabeth. Her reaction was not quite what he had hoped for.

'I would have thought,' she remarked seriously after one small smile, 'that you'd have to diagnose them before you forgave them, not the other way round.' Then she proceeded to quote a line of, to Gareth, quite unfamiliar invective, which she said was poetry, but which all the same included a word Gareth was mildly shocked to hear her say.

At the same time he was impressed by her ability to use such words so unselfconsciously. It had sounded unselfconscious, at any rate, though on the whole he rather hoped the unselfconsciousness was assumed, since you would never know where you were, he thought, with a girl who could use words like that without even trying.

His disapproval evidently showed, because Elizabeth, mistaking its cause, asked, 'Don't you think it's true, then?'

'No, not really. Not for me, at any rate. My mother did her best for me, I can't really expect any more than that, can I?'

'But that's what the poem means. He's saying, the poet,

that whatever they do, however hard they try their best, they'll still do something very wrong somewhere, d'you see?'

Gareth shrugged. 'You know what I think: it doesn't really matter that much what they do, so long as they love you,' he said. There, that'll shut her up for a bit, he thought, watching her as she sighed, picked up her glass, and took a slow reflective sip. He had noticed long before that direct references to Love disconcerted Elizabeth, impressed and even thrilled her, since she herself spoke of relationships, family situations, terms of acceptance, and role models. She can say Fuck without thinking about it, thought Gareth fondly, but she can't say Love. No wonder she loves me.

He remembered their first real date. Elizabeth had been attached then to two psychiatric wards, and was not enjoying the work.

'We just don't seem to be doing anything to help them,' she had complained over her rainbow-trout-with-almonds, 'they just sit there, rocking backwards and forwards, or twitching, or chain-smoking. All we've done is herd them together, like a, like a leper colony. We don't do anything to help them, not really.'

'But there is no help for them,' Gareth had replied commiseratingly, though his own experience of psychiatry had bored rather than distressed him. 'You can't take their childhoods away, you can't take their memories away.' As he spoke he had realized excitedly that he believed what he was saying, that he had discovered an immense truth, comically simple, as truths often seem.

'You can't take their childhoods away from them,' he repeated. 'Don't you see that they're crazy because they've never been loved properly: when they were babies, when they were children, even when they were conceived maybe, they just weren't loved enough. That's about the worst thing that can happen to a human being, and when it happens to you, you grow up into a nutter, unless perhaps you're extra strong, abnormally strong. And these people, your patients, they were weak, d'you see, ordinary and weak to begin with. And so they're crazy, and there's nothing you can do about it.'

His sincerity had made him tremble as he spoke; made Elizabeth fall unhesitatingly in love with him; indeed they had hurried through the rest of the meal almost speechless with passion, so greatly had his daring no-holds-barred references to Love excited them both. And for weeks afterwards his revelation had elated him: he had stumbled, he felt, across one of the beliefs that made up his claim to adulthood.

Though this had happened nearly a year before, and the theory was now so familiar that he privately doubted both its truth and its originality. Gareth and Elizabeth were often irritated with one another lately. As now.

'I'm very fond of my parents,' said Elizabeth at last, 'but that doesn't mean to say I can't criticize them.' She was immediately annoyed with herself for saying this. It was not what she really meant at all, though when she had given the words their quick mental check-over they had seemed near enough. Aloud they were limp with adolescence. Elizabeth picked up a swag of her brown hair and began to look through it.

Gareth's mind slipped back to Wilde. 'But will you forgive them?' he asked her teasingly. Whatever the argument was about, he felt that she was losing it, and so he was prepared to be affectionate.

'I don't know yet,' said Elizabeth smartly, 'I'm not old enough.'

'So long as you do it before you get to be, say, twenty-five. I think everyone should have forgiven their parents by then. There'd be something really wrong with someone who hadn't forgiven his parents at that age.'

'Or something really wrong with the parents.' Elizabeth

caught a split end, separated it from the rest, and neatly executed it.

'No, no.' Gareth thought of their first date. 'Either you forgive them, or they're so awful you can't forgive them. And if they're that awful, if they're really that bad, it means they haven't loved you properly, and so you're a nutter! And probably not worth knowing. That's what I mean. Either you forgive them, or you're not worth knowing, 'cause you're a nutter, see?' he finished in stage Cockney, in case Elizabeth took his words too seriously. He was not sure how strongly he could defend his position if she did.

'See?' he repeated, after a pause. Elizabeth had found another split end, a real beauty, as multi-branched as a little Christmas tree. She felled it.

'Sounds a big dogmatic,' she said at last.

Gareth looked at her doubtfully. Could it be, he asked himself, could it be that she was *bored*?

'Good therapy, is that?'

'Why? Does it get on your nerves?'

'It does, a bit,' said Gareth apologetically.

'Helps me resist direct eye-contact,' said Elizabeth with her sly smile.

'That must be very useful,' Gareth smiled back. 'Want another drink?'

When he came back from the bar he felt that the un-pleasant tension between them had dissolved. Gareth moved his chair further round the little table so that they sat closer together.

'Hallo,' he said.

'Hallo.'

He sought about for some interesting and uncontroversial topic.

'Did I ever tell you,' he began, 'about the Brain Tumour Man?'

'No,' said Elizabeth guardedly.

'Well then. This'll help you. Listen to this, see what you make of it.'

'All right.' He often turns our conversations into teaching sessions, thought Elizabeth. She wondered if this were altogether a healthy sign. Whatever shall we talk about when I'm qualified? But no doubt, she concluded bleakly, we shall have parted before then.

'Early forties,' said Gareth enjoyably, 'male, married, two kids. Classic symptoms, real textbook stuff: sudden terrible headaches, worst in the mornings; sudden onset of difficulties with fine movements –' Gareth tapped his right forefinger and thumb together to indicate what the Brain Tumour Man had been unable to manage – 'and very sudden (morning of admission) onset of Jacksonian fits, beginning with his left hand, quiver quiver quiver!'

Gareth demonstrated, with some eyeball rolling, the prolonged clonic extremities of Jacksonian convulsion: they sat in quite a dark corner of the pub.

'Gareth, please,' said Elizabeth, not amused. In her mind she had made the Brain Tumour Man in the likeness of the vicar at home, a nice inoffensive soul whose sufferings must not be mocked.

'So what d'you do?' asked Gareth, slightly abashed, though he knew he did rather a good Jacksonian convulsion. 'What d'you do?'

'A lumbar puncture. A CAT-scan.'

'Very good, yes, excellent,' said Gareth warmly. 'I did a lumbar puncture, but it was O.K. And booked a CAT-scan and a bronchoscopy to see if he had anything nasty in his lungs. But he never got any of that lot, because as soon as he was admitted, he started to have generalized convulsions, status epilepticus, the real McCoy.'

Elizabeth's vicar's wife, a little child on either hand, sobbed in the waiting-room as the vicar's fits rattled the bars of his iron hospital bed.

'Oh dear,' said Elizabeth.

'Nothing we could do,' said Gareth. 'Nothing we could do at all. It was like *2001*. You remember that part where the astronaut slowly dismantles the computer, unlocks its brains bit by bit?'

'Yes, terrible . . .'

'This man was like that. You felt you could almost see the tumour in his brain, see it growing, blotting out the centres one by one, memory, speech, movement, hearing. One by one. Like the stars going out.'

There was a pause, while each enjoyed that mixture of human involvement and clinical know-how that makes medical shop-talk so satisfying.

'Must have been highly malignant.'

'Oh yes, highly malignant,' agreed Gareth cheerfully. 'But this is the really interesting part. I had to go to the post-mortem to do the report. So. The chap does his chopper-work, you know. Looks through the brain, this is going to be easy, looks through the brain, flick flick flick.' Gareth briefly mimed someone leafing through the pages of a book. 'And there we all stood, all waiting. And waiting. And waiting. There was a sort of social embarrassment in the air, none of us meeting one another's eyes. Because there was nothing there. Nothing at all. No trace of tumour anywhere. Nothing anywhere else either.'

'But that's – what killed him then?'

Ah, she was impressed at last, thought Gareth happily. 'God knows,' he replied aloud. 'Really, God knows, because we don't.' He shook his head gravely as he reached for his beer. A thrilling story too, if just a tiny bit altered to fit the framework he had seen would suit it best. A story of the old dispute between Science and Nature, a story in which he was himself nicely depicted as a young initiate of Science still broadminded enough to point out Nature's occasional baffling victories.

Here the not-quite-conscious train of Gareth's thought came abruptly to a halt, as if somewhere some alert internal signalman had blown a whistle. Gareth looked backwards, inspecting the tracks. What had happened? Some thought had nudged him. He frowned, concentrating, and slowly the nudge formed words: I thought I was telling the story because it was interesting, but really I told it because it made me look good, and in a very subtle way, a way she might not even consciously notice.

And the thought had general application, as such thoughts often did: could self-aggrandizement be behind all his stories, Gareth wondered. Could it be behind everyone's stories? The family myths and legends Jessie had so often told him, or stories swopped in pubs, or over coffee at work, or after dinner?

After-dinner stories. Could it be that all of them, even jokes, even 'I read in the paper this morning' were told with some deeper unconscious purpose, told in order to construct a personality in the teller? Perhaps we choose our stories, thought Gareth, as we choose different clothes, or the things we hang on the walls. So, and so I told Elizabeth about the Brain Tumour Man because she would be impressed with me, or . . .

His thought trailed away in confusion. Had he really made any discovery after all? Perhaps he had simply come across the obvious, fallen over it so suddenly that he had not immediately recognized it for what it was. Gareth glanced quickly across the table at Elizabeth, and considered sharing the thought with her. She would be sure to do so herself, had the idea been her own. She was like that, he thought sourly. It was a function, after all, of class. Only the assured middle classes could repeat imaginative fancies without fear.

'Perhaps it was a ghost,' Elizabeth broke in.

'What?'

'A brain tumour ghost. The shade of an astrocytoma. Got in and killed him. You know,' said Elizabeth as Gareth continued to look blank, 'your Brain Tumour Man.'

'Oh. Yes.' There, what did I tell you, he asked his inner self rhetorically. A function of class.

Scowling he downed the rest of his pint in silence, and Elizabeth, turning disconsolately back to her split ends, imagined telling her unattached friend of her suspicions: I feel he's, you know, emotionally having me on; I keep wondering, Is this real, or is it another affectation? He just can't be trusted.

Or am I, Elizabeth less enjoyably asked herself, just fed up with him? But then, if she were to drop him, she would have no one to go out with, no one to have a drink with or see a film with; she might get just like the unattached friend, who had recently developed a habit of lying on her bed in the dark every evening, listening to Radio Four.

Perhaps I should try to hang onto him, Elizabeth thought, until something better turns up.

The stern inner voice of feminism hissed for shame, and presently Elizabeth wore much the same scowl as Gareth; and so Gareth's last untroubled evening for many a long week passed uncomfortably away.

EIGHT

JOAN, Cissie and Jessie sat in the relatives' waiting-room, and waited. The door was open, and brief hospital scenes, like pictures in a sideshow, flashed by along the corridor outside, with a full accompaniment of hospital noises: porters with rattling empty trolleys, and once with a creaking full one, which bore a shallow pile of blankets shaped like a woman, with two bright living eyes at one end, and two stiff fat little feet at the other; the blood-collecting lady, pricking by on her high heels, rattling her tray of shiny glass bottles; the black ward domestic, holding by its long drooping neck the ward vacuum cleaner, the body of which dragged the ground behind her like a small dead dinosaur; nurses, all sizes, shapes and colours, serious, busy, giggling, and once in tears; a small herd of medical men at the heels of a large bald lewd-eyed fat man in a beautiful grey suit, who carried in one hand a cardboard cake-box tied with green ribbons; and other more anonymous personnel, the bit-players of hospital life, students, cleaners' supervisors, two broad-shouldered young women hauling a large green cylinder about, and a man with a beard and elastic-banded pony-tail, holding an empty wooden tea-tray in either hand.

Once, too, came the full-scale infantry-charge noises of

an emergency admission; many running feet, a demented chorus of high-speed squeaking trolley wheels, smothered yells of command, with at last a horrid glimpse of more human-shaped blankets, all hung about with glistening tubes and pudgy bags of dripping fluid, while all the nurses' telephones, it seemed, rang at once.

Worse were the smells, blown by with each set of passing footsteps: school dinner smells like hot steamed cloth, talcum powder, air fresheners, simple shit and ageing urine, floor wax and chilly disinfectant.

These smells spoke of something uncontrolled, even abandoned. Human substances were here unchecked, split, handled. Here an endless war waged, over territory and equipment; not in the usual way, over rights of possession, but in the hospital way, over levels of cleanliness. The geriatrics dribbled and seeped: the nurses replied with Dettol, Glitto, and the fierce jets of aerosol cans. Ancients worn out by the battle were always replaced ('No empty beds tonight again,' the night nurse might gasp over the telephone to her supervisor, six nights out of seven) while the young nurses, after a hectic eight-week tour of duty, are replaced and sent back to Blighty more or less unharmed.

'We could shut the door,' murmured Jessie, after half-an-hour's exposure, 'couldn't we?' But to touch, let alone change, anything in this terrible place seemed as out of the question as complaining about the Ladies' on arrival in Hell.

And so the three sat in fidgety silence for another fifteen minutes, at the end of which period a young doctor looked in, stepped in, and shut the door behind her. She was small, plump, and pale with exhaustion. On today's page of her notebook, following a score of duties already met, was written, 'Lorrigan – rels'. Only forty minutes late, thought the doctor, which wasn't too bad at all really, what with the emergency admission and all. She turned her red-rimmed eyes on the Lorrigan rels, who shifted nervously in their chairs as one woman, and she spoke, as follows:

'Sorry I'm late. You're here for Mrs Lily Lorrigan. Yes? Well, she's going to do very well, we think. She's shaken of course, but no bones broken. Now I know she doesn't recognize anyone, and I can understand you being upset. But this confusion is very natural at this stage. She's an old lady in a strange place. It's almost certain to wear off very soon. So try not to worry too much, O.K.? Any questions now?'

An amiable and practised speech, which her audience received in complete silence. They had no questions. They slowly shook their heads, eyeing one another. No questions.

'Well, in that case – I'll see you later, I expect, good morning!'

Only Jessie managed to articulate a 'Thank you, goodbye!' while Cissie opened her mouth silently and Joan looked hopelessly at the carpet without making any effort to speak at all.

The young doctor softly closed the door behind her, ticked off Lorrigan's rels, and pounded off to duties new.

In the waiting-room, Cissie was the first to speak. 'Wool,' she whispered to Jessie, 'what did she say?'

The truth was that all three sisters had heard a different speech, for doctors, like many other professional beings, are apt to speak in tongues. Often they are unaware of this gift, and can be heard complaining to one another over lunch: 'Spent twenty minutes explaining what an oesophagoscopy is, and today the old twerp says, "But where do you make the cut, doctor?" I don't know why I bother, it's a waste of my time *and* theirs . . .'

The nature of the gift is, that whatever the doctor says sounds like something else to the patient, and like something else again to the patient's rels. No matter how clearly the words are spoken, how carefully they are chosen, passage through the air irretrievably garbles them.

As a further complication, a patient's hearing may be so affected by fear that, while misinterpreting much of what the doctor says, he simply cannot hear the rest; and what does actually penetrate may well slip completely away in the common amnesia of terror.

So it was that Jessie, who was able to concentrate fairly well on the young doctor's words due to having a flesh-and-blood relation in the same professional camp, heard nearly all of the speech as it was spoken, though the extra scare of the doctor's sex lost her a few words here and there. While Cissie heard the doctor say:

'We *think* she'll be all right. Badly shaken of course. She doesn't recognize anyone. Naturally. She's very old. But there's no point in worrying about it. And that's your lot.'

While Joan clearly, if fleetingly, heard:

'She might be all right. We can't be sure. But she's very badly shaken. Of course she doesn't recognize you, you're to blame, aren't you? She's very old and ill, but why should *you* worry? Now take yourself off.' Joan had forgotten all this, however, before the door had properly closed, remembering only the doctor's tone, which to her had been condemnatory, even a snarl. So she looked up with a faint stir of hope when Cissie spoke.

'Wool, what did she say?'

Jessie considered. 'Not so bad, then,' she offered tentatively, ready to withdraw if anyone else, hearing different meanings, demanded indignantly, What you mean, not so bad!

But no one did.

'Could of been a lot worse,' said Cissie, also very carefully. There was a pause.

'Got to expect it at her age,' Jessie went on. She rose and patted Joan's arm. 'Come on, buck up. No bones broken, that's the main thing.'

Joan, under this encouragement, hit on her own formula at last: 'It'll never happen again, I can promise you that.'

Murmuring and patting one another, Cissie, Joan and

Jessie made their halting way along the hospital corridor, down the stone stairs and out into the bright, loud, moving morning air.

'Cuppa tea, I reckon,' said Cissie, nodding her head towards a sign across the street.

'Where?' Jessie followed the direction of Cissie's eyes, saw orange net curtains and a black man sitting at a table by the window. 'Oh, not *there*, d'you mean?'

'Wool, yeah,' replied Cissie ashamedly, ''course it's a bit of a dive, but, just for a cuppa, wool, I can see it's a bit of a dive –' Jessie's ability to speak to the young lady doctor had quite demoralized Cissie.

Jessie hesitated. Cissie handed over the reins so rarely that it was hard to know how to behave when she did; though Cissie held them, Jessie felt, only as long as she, Jessie, allowed her to. It was a great deal less trouble to let Cissie feel that she was in charge, and often no trouble at all to push her, as it were from behind, in Jessie's own preferred direction. Jessie had avoided many childhood difficulties by allowing Cissie the sensation of power. And no one had ever seen where the truth lay, a joke Jessie had savoured, if not quite consciously, for more than forty years.

Perhaps it was with some mild desire to protect the old pose of Cissie-as-leader that Jessie now turned to Joan and asked diffidently,

'What do you want to do, Joanie?'

'What, me?'

'D'you want a cup of tea over there? No, over there, see?'

'Oh. Oh, yes. Yes, please.'

Though it was hardly likely that anyone who knew her would happen past, Jessie took the precaution of herding her sisters towards the dim back corner of the café, to a table as far from the window as possible.

'There.' Jessie pulled her good leather gloves off, finger-tip by fingertip, which she knew was the correct way to remove gloves, and laid them palm-to-palm upon the formica table, after first stroking it with one hand to make sure it was dry and crumb-free.

'Take your coat off, Joan.' Jessie resisted a strong temptation to lean over and help her sister with the buttons. 'Tea all round? Cissie?'

Cissie had noticed being herded. Mentally she rehearsed Jessie's refined high-pitched dismay for Jeff's future entertainment and her own revenge: 'Ooaw, not they-er!' She had quite forgotten the Goodbye. Her eyes glinted.

'Three teas, please,' said Jessie to the elderly woman in slippers who had slouched over to their table. The waitress wore an orange nylon coatee, stained brownish at the front over her stomach, which part she leant against the table as if to relieve herself of its protuberant weight. Jessie looked away as she ordered.

'I want something to eat,' said Cissie loudly. 'Got buttered buns?'

The waitress nodded.

'What about you, Joan, you ought to have something, two buttered buns, please,' Cissie said.

The waitress turned inquiringly to Jessie, who shook her head. Well, that didn't last long, thought Jessie, without excitement. So as not to seem defiant she avoided Cissie's eyes, which she knew would be fixed upon her, and looked around at the other tables, but casually, lest her very avoidance be seen as a challenge.

What she saw did not much comfort her. Beside the counter sat two old men who looked like tramps, one with white hair sticking out from beneath a blue beret like a Frenchman's. They were both smoking little stubs of hand-rolled cigarettes. Jessie remembered her own father smoking these and spitting out the dabs of wet dissolving paper and tobacco shreds that stuck to his lips. Tramps weren't so bad, poor things, thought Jessie. She had a vague notion that tramps were all shell-shocked soldiers, First World

War soldiers like her father, and all too damaged to rest. No, tramps weren't so bad.

But well, *blacks*. The one by the window. Two shiny fat girls halfway in, near the tramps. And a man with a turban two tables away. They made the place look so untidy, thought Jessie. Even squalid. It's not that I've got racial prejudice. No. It's just that they make a place look so untidy.

There was another dark face behind the counter. 'What's he, d'you think?' she asked Cissie, moving her eyes to show whom she meant. Being questioned mollified Cissie still further, as Jessie had intended.

Cissie turned round in her chair.

'Him? Greek Cypriot,' she said with complete conviction. She turned round again and stared hard at the slender young man, as if daring him to be anything else, and presently, after a short, startled glance back at her, the young man withdrew to the shelter of his own tea urn, and disappeared behind it.

The buns arrived. Ready buttered, noticed Jessie with revulsion. She herself preferred the neat little pats of butter, all individually wrapped and fresh from the fridge, that the proper places served.

'Sugar?' asked the waitress. No sugar on the tables! Jessie shook her head, trying not to look at the propped stomach.

'Two for me and one for her,' said Cissie cheerfully.

'Feeling better?' Jessie turned to Joan.

'I come here,' said Joan happily, 'with a friend.' She liked the sound of 'a friend'. If you said 'my friend' or 'Dierdre' it looked as if you only had the one. Whereas 'a friend' sounded as if you had dozens. The café's familiarity had cheered her up, and it was nice to think that she had some little thing in life that neither Jessie nor Cissie knew about or shared in.

'When we've been to the museum,' she went on.

Jessie remembered something about Cissie's eldest, and, what was it? Dollshouses? She caught Cissie's eye, looking up just as Cissie did, and they exchanged a certain resigned and comradely look.

'That's nice,' Jessie told Joan, brightly.

'I usually sit by the window. The people go past, you can watch them, once I saw a funny thing: a black man, very tall, wearing all these long white robes, all billowing down to the ground, all majestic. And then I saw his feet, he had slippers on, pretend leopard skin. Bedroom slippers, all furry. It's true.'

Jessie marvelled politely.

'And not before time,' said Cissie to the elderly waitress as the teas arrived. A few heads turned; she had spoken loudly.

Jessie lowered her eyes and looked at her own smart leather handbag in her lap. She had a sudden memory of Cissie in her teens, publicly squeezing her spots in front of the kitchen mirror, and leaving the little yellow plugs all clinging to the glass afterwards. She's never tried to better herself, thought Jessie stroking her handbag, and she's never even wanted to. Jessie saw that she had thus placed a memory, hooked it up to the present and made it mean something, and was comforted.

'Here. I got an idea,' said Cissie, stirring her tea so that the spoon made a little clinking noise against the side of the cup. From earliest infancy all Lily's children heard Lily do this, and so they all did it too, the sound being an integral part of the comfort of tea.

'Ooh, a really good idea,' grinned Cissie, over the trio of clinking spoons.

'Well?'

'It's – while Mum's in the hospital. We all get together, the whole family. And do the place up. Clean it. Do it all up.'

There was a short silence.

'What, you mean, redecorate?' asked Jessie, putting her teaspoon down.

'Yeah, yeah, do it all up! Jeff do the garden, the men all do the garden. Us the inside. Wash the carpets –'

'They'd come to bits,' said Jessie darkly.

Cissie ignored her. 'It needs a real good turn-out, that place. Full of junk. I don't mean no offence,' Cissie added, turning to Joan. 'No offence. The place is too big to deal with all on your own, what with doing Mum and all.'

Joan was silent, wondering whether she ought to be offended or not.

'It *is* a lot for me to deal with,' she agreed tentatively. The thought had not occurred to her before.

''Course it is, 'course it is,' cried Cissie, who seemed to have quite forgotten her usual position on Joan's ministrations to Lily, ''course it is, God knows how Mum and Dad ever ended up with a place that big, three storeys, and there's that damp bit on the landing, Jeff could do that. And the stairs. We didn't do the stairs last time, did we, remember? Must've been before the War that place got done up last.'

'It's a disgrace,' murmured Jessie. She saw herself humming in the car down to London every evening after work, or even taking a week off, and covering her hair with a fresh red scarf with white dots on it. She saw herself laughing, with a paint roller in one hand.

'Oh, let's do it,' she cried warmly.

Joan pondered.

'Be a fresh start for Mum,' said Cissie, knowing she was on to a winner. 'Fresh start for her after her accident, eh, Joanie?'

Cissie herself was entranced by her visions: matching curtains and bedcovers, Crafty Space Savers, a Unique Saucepan Holder. She would wear an old but becoming shirt of Jeff's, smock-like and slimming.

'What you say, Joan? it's your own home after all,' Cissie added, in case this had occurred to Joan herself, and thus spiking her guns if it had.

But Joan was making coffee for everyone, being cheered by a busy friendly crowd as she entered with her steaming tray. She would need mugs. On television people always drank out of mugs when they were decorating. She would have to get some at Sainsbury's, cheap pretty ones. The cashier would stare at all those mugs being bought at once. She might ask, Having a party? And Joan would smile and reply, In a way.

'It's her own home after all,' Cissie told Jessie, as Joan remained silent.

'Well?' asked Jessie.

'All right,' said Joan.

Jessie clapped her hands.

'Oh, lovely, lovely,' cried Cissie, 'I *am* looking forward to it.' Something to do now the wedding was over. Funny how you missed it, she thought, all that worry too.

'So, who'll be doing it?' Jessie counted on her fingers. 'Us three, of course. Jeff. Your two lads, Cis, –'

'Not Marion, she's out,' Cissie went on. 'Not Jim –' Jimmy was on a late holiday, touring rainy Scotland, with another fortnight still to go. 'What about *your* lad?' Cissie asked Jessie, faintly sarcastic.

'Well, he doesn't get very much time to himself, you know, as it is, I know he'd like to help, I'll ask him, but honestly I can't see it, he'll be sorry about it I know.'

Cissie sniffed at this bluster. 'So that's six of us,' she announced. 'Shouldn't take too long if we all do our bit.'

'Can't take too long,' Joan put in, 'because Mum won't be in hospital that long, will she?'

'Of course she won't,' said Jessie.

Cissie was silent. She had suddenly remembered what she had told Jimmy's Carol about Jessie's Gareth. So long as Jimmy and Carol were safely in Scotland, and Mum in hospital, nothing could get passed on, she decided. It wouldn't do to have Jessie going off in a huff now.

To placate the huffy Jessie she had imagined, Cissie allowed Jessie to pay the bill when it at length arrived.

Though presently, outside, she felt recovered enough to insist on paying all the tube fares home.

NINE

GARETH sat alone in a pub in Soho, and worked on his plan of campaign. After the first numbing shock of it – and how could he have failed to foresee the problem? – he had determined to stay calm and think out all the possible consequences of Lily's hospitalization and what, if anything, he could do about them.

Clearly the major question was, would anyone connect the foul-mouthed old hag with himself? He took out his work notebook and turned to a clean page.

Must not connect, he wrote quickly, and underlined the words. They looked a little familiar. Must not connect. But I've no time for that sort of thing now, thought Gareth, making a shrug-face into his beer. He turned his thoughts back to the old hag in question, and his conscience made a small, irritant complaint as he did so.

Isn't she my own grandmother after all?

Gareth slightly shook his head. Nope. Can't get me that way. If she was more – if she was different – if she was a proper presentable grandmother, something between, say, Lady Bracknell and Mrs Palfrey at the Claremont; or if she were, even, a loveable if spirited old Cockney of the Old Dear/Irene Handl variety, no one, thought Gareth, would be more filial than he. But she wasn't Lady Bracknell and Mrs Palfrey; she was Sairey Gamp and Madame Defarge.

Had she not physically abused his own mother in childhood? A superannuated baby-batterer! No call to pity such a uniquely unattractive person merely because she was a blood-relation and grown old. No call at all.

Nor would she be a model patient. Oh dear, no. She'd have a wonderful time, once she recovered a little. Four or five nurses a shift, many of them inexperienced young girls: four or five Joans to torment. She would be an incessant bell-ringer, an incompetent bed-pan user (Oops sorry, nurse) a night-moaner, a non-compliant medication-taker, a meal-rejecter. And she would bite. Her kind always did. Teeth or no, she would snap her gums at the nurses like an angry old tortoise.

No, there must be no connection.

What to do Gareth wrote next.

1. Steer clear of her.

There could be no visits, of course. Easy enough to smooth things over with Jessie: his job was tailor-made for deceit. 'I got called in,' or 'there was an emergency.' Emergencies would always see him through visiting-time. Of course everyone else would expect him to pop up to see her whenever he could, visiting-time or no, as he worked (curses) in the same hospital.

And that was no problem either, Gareth told himself stoutly. She was fairly comatose presently, if Jessie was anything to go by. Funny how she sounded exactly like Aunt Cissie over the telephone. What do I sound like over the telephone?

Stop that. Keep to the question in hand. Now then, thought Gareth to himself reasonably, easy enough to give out that I've nipped up to see her dozens of times, and that she didn't recognize me. Which would account for any awkward claims the old hag might make later on when she came to.

When she perked up, if she perked up, he would merely alter the story a little. 'Popped up during my lunchbreak but she was asleep,' or in the bathroom or being seen by the House Officer. He could go on indefinitely. Or perhaps not indefinitely, but certainly for a good long while.

2. *If she talks.*

Would Lily, in the sea-change of hospitalization, grow friendly and chat to the nurses? Old ladies always nattered so. Especially during those long, ritualistic blanket-baths all nurses seemed to go in for. Lily had a sweet smile when she felt like using it. After a week of being ministered to, might she not, to interest or impress the nurses, say confidingly, 'I got a grandson works here'?

Disaster.

But wait. What would the nurse say?

'Oh really? What's his name?'

Ha! Gareth struck his fist lightly on the table, so that his beer trembled. She won't know what my surname is. It was exactly the sort of thing she would forget. She never wrote letters these days. His father had been dead for years. There was at least a sporting chance that she had last heard Jessie's new surname at Jessie's own wedding.

On the other hand – Gareth picked up his beer. My Christian name. She'd have to be bloody senile to forget that too.

'Gareth?' the nurse might ask, musing. 'D'you mean Dr Williams?'

'Williams, thass it. Knew it was summink Welsh,' Lily would smirk from her pillows.

There was simply nothing he could do if she identified him. Except own up, as quickly as possible, and appear unabashed, or people would imagine – people being what they were – that he was ashamed of her, out of pure snobbery. Which was not so, Gareth thought, indignantly. It had simply been absolutely necessary to cut himself off from the family, because they were passive and feckless; because they were the people who had things done to them, who were governed, conscripted: people who read the label *100% real nylon* and felt reassured. That was them. And I won't be made to feel one of them, no, never.

All the same, no one must imagine that he was ashamed of Lily or her kin; if anyone thought him a dishonourable snob, he would, somehow, be one.

And it certainly wouldn't do to think too closely about that one, Gareth decided, moving quickly onto:

3. Mother.

Would she blab? He tried to imagine Jessie telling the ward staff about her boy. No. No, she was more subtle than that. More likely to arrange things, somehow, so that people asked her what her son did. She wouldn't want to seem unduly proud of him; that would lessen her own status, and, she would recognize, his too. And she wouldn't want that. She had her own struggles with her background. No, on the whole he could count on her to keep quiet. But there would still be

4. Aunt Cissie

Who was never troubled with subtlety. She would claim him outright. 'My nephew, he –' as soon as Jessie, with her more immediate claims, was safely out of earshot.

Would she, like Lily, forget his name? Gareth considered. She'd remember. No point in hoping otherwise. She'd remember it all right, when she needed to. Peasant cunning, that's what she had. Low peasant cunning. And she'd notice *1.* if no one else did. She would notice, and draw conclusions. Beside note number four he added, *Keep her sweet*.

He rose and went to the bar with his empty glass.

'Same again, please.' The pub was very quiet. Fills up when the theatres empty, I suppose, thought Gareth. Back in his seat he looked about himself, musing.

Keeping Cissie sweet.

But how?

For a while he watched the three young men who had sat

down at the small round table next to his own. All three had eager, ageing young faces and clothes a little out of the ordinary. The most dominant, Gareth noticed, wore a long black cloak and black and pink striped socks. Arty types, thought Gareth scornfully. He eavesdropped, discerning Cambridge in the open-ended 'Yahs' of agreement.

'Yah, but must we compromise the *British* structure of . . .'

Of what, of what, thought Gareth crossly. He felt sure none of the three had wildly embarrassing ancestors all set to ruin their public images. At this moment, one of the young men, perhaps feeling Gareth's eyes, turned a little and flashed him an unmistakeable smile.

Gareth looked away blushing, pretending not to have noticed. His heart beat fast. He felt outraged and flattered. After a time he became annoyed with himself for feeling pleased, and remembered that he would soon lose Elizabeth for ever. She wouldn't understand his position; she would draw all the obvious conclusions – so unfairly! – and finish with him, not because of Lily, but because he had kept quiet about her. So she would say, anyway.

Elizabeth! She would leave him for ever, and he would have to sit in pubs all alone, and strange young men would make disquieting gestures at him.

Concentrate, he told himself grimly. Number four, keeping Cissie sweet. Concentrate. Keeping the whole lot of them sweet.

Gareth sat up straight suddenly. Wait a minute! he thought. What else had Jessie said over the telephone, in her ardent Cockney? They were going to decorate. That condemned old house. Where Lily lived.

Of course! Gareth narrowed his eyes. I could show up a few times. Maybe swop a few on-calls and turn up a fair number of times. They'd love it. They'd love me. And if after all they blabbed, he would be able to answer anyone's accusing eyes, even Elizabeth's, with 'Yes, I've been helping to redecorate her house for her, poor old love, she's not herself of course, she's usually such a dear old thing.'

A handy line to have in reserve, should need arise. And Jessie would be delighted, and so should his conscience.

I quite like decorating, too.

Gareth saw himself manfully scaling a ladder in the dizzy old stairwell. He could wear that old pair of jeans, the tight pair with the patch on one knee.

He remembered Marion's wedding and how he had tempted the Fates by admitting to happiness. Gareth sighed, and when the young man at the next table once more caught his eye and tentatively smiled, he purposely refrained from scowling back in reply, because after all you could never really tell whose side the Fates were on.

TEN

IN the early hours of the next morning, as she slept, Lily began that series of small internal adjustments which would shortly lead to her death.

She looked serene enough, and well-cared for, inside the flowered hospital nightie and smooth white sheets. So far the heart attack she had suffered during her fall had given no trouble at all; no trouble to anyone.

The wounded part had floundered a little at first, missing beats and confusedly trying to make up for them by throwing in a few extras all bundled together; but by the time the ambulance arrived the first crisis was over, and by the time Lily arrived at the hospital something quite indistinguishable from normal service had been resumed.

Sleeping Lily dreamt that she was watching a tennis match; unconcernedly suspended, like the television cameras, in mid-air, she watched a mixed-doubles contest with mild interest, and ate salted cockles from a small white china saucer she held in one hand. It was all nice enough, as dreams went.

Meanwhile her injured heart, growing tired, pumped more feebly, and Lily's blood, instead of hurtling smoothly through and away to Lily's arterial highways, was forced to form a sort of liquid queue to get by.

Lily dreamt that the tennis players were using live hamsters for tennis balls, and twitched uneasily in her sleep.

The liquid queue lengthened by slow degrees, became a serious traffic jam. Lily's coronary vessels thronged and jostled, distended with blood. At last normal procedures became out of the question and fluid, having nowhere else to go, began to diffuse through into Lily's lungs from certain swollen vessels.

Lily dreamt that one of the hamsters had been whacked splosh into a nearby pond, and that she had been commanded to dive in and retrieve it, although she had explained to everyone that she couldn't swim. But the pool opened itself up right beside her, so she had no choice but to leap in, and fell down and down into its cold blue depths through the clear panels of sunlight to the dark deep bottom, where a tennis ball lay just within her grasp. Clutching it Lily struck out for the surface, but found herself immobile; with a great burst of terror she found that she was being held down at the pool's depths, held firmly despite her frantic struggles, while the heavy soft water pressed suffocatingly all about her.

Lily looked less peaceful now. She kicked her bedclothes about and occasionally knocked her hands against the padded cot-sides strapped to her bed to keep her safe within.

Lily's lungs continued to fill with fluid. She breathed more quickly, trying to compensate for the loss, but still she was taking in less oxygen. Her nightmares became vaguer, and continuous. The roses on the stairwell wallpaper at home grew teeth and snapped at her; needles made threatening noises; the patterns of old familiar pieces of cloth rose and fought sickening battles before her eyes.

At last Lily's brain became so starved of oxygen that,

losing all normal controls, it presented Lily with an extensive and well-developed psychosis. Crazed Lily snapped awake: it was time to die. She struggled up sideways, her ears full of roaring and thudding noises, and came up against the padded cot-sides. They were a problem, annoying but not insoluble, Lily felt. While she pondered, the air-raid siren lifted up its voice and wailed. Lily managed to hook one knee over the left-hand cot-side and was doing her best with the other leg when, to her immense surprise, since he should have been back at work by now, she saw her husband washing his hands at the kitchen sink.

'Hey!' called Lily. There he was, small sandy man, standing beside the bed wearing a small cool smile like the Mona Lisa's, though his version was studded as usual with a hand-rolled cigarette, which glowed a brilliant red through the gloom

'What you doing here?' Lily cried aloud.

He made no answer. Instead he crept crab-like over the cot-sides and sat on Lily's stomach. Lily was outraged.

'Here, what're you – stop that! Stoppit!'

He only smiled more broadly and leant forward, pressing with all his weight on Lily's chest, so that it was almost impossible for her to breathe.

'Stop that, get off me!' gasped Lily, beginning to struggle as violently as she could.

Her husband went on smiling, and when he spoke, he used a soft girl's voice to mock Lily with:

'Now then, Mrs Lorrigan. Wake up dear, what's the matter?'

'Get away, you bastard!' shouted Lily, and took a fierce swipe at the air. Her hand connected; there was a small surprised squeal somewhere to Lily's right.

'Leave me alone, oh, help, help, Joanie!'

'Put the light on,' replied Lily's husband in his soft urgent woman's voice, 'and call Julia, will you?'

Joan, a little skinny girl again, poked her nose over the cot-side and rolled her eyes, 'Can I come, Mum?'

Lily's husband went on smiling. He lifted one hand and began to fumble Lily's nightdress with it. His fingers touched her old empty breast, with a touch as cold as a ring of steel. Lily screamed loudly again and again.

'Is this oxygen on?' The chill hand withdrew. Lights flashed and a crowd of people ran heavily round in circles.

Something wrapped itself over Lily's mouth and nose, clamped itself on like a murderer's broad hand. Lily fought it, twisting her head about.

'Lasix, and a stat E.C.G. please.'

'Should we catheterize her?'

'Oh yes. Yes please. Indwelling. Hourly output.'

'Nice deep breaths, Lily.'

'Sit her up again, will you?'

'Big deep breaths, that's a good girl, in, and out, and in, and out, that's very good . . .'

Hauled upright, Lily abruptly stopped dying.

She fell asleep again, and her dreams cheered up nicely.

She was playing in the sand-pit in the park. Her mother was going to buy her an ice-cream.

'Good girl, deep breaths, that's a good girl, feeling better now, Lily?'

'Sand,' said dreaming Lily, and smiled in her sleep.

ELEVEN

A WEEK had passed. It was Friday evening again, and Joan and Cissie had made a start on the front room. Everything had really gone quite well, considering, so well that tonight, with the extra pleasures of the weekend drawing near, Cissie, from being high-spirited, became quite uproarious.

'Look, watch. This is what them artists do. See! Splat!' and from a distance of several feet she flung her soapy washcloth at the wall, where it instantly spread a spiky blot of moisture before bouncing away onto the floor.

'See that, Art they call that, do it with paint, chuck it at the canvas, monkeys do it!' Still chuckling she picked up the cloth and smacked it hard against the wallpaper, marking it with splayed wedge-shaped prints, so that a frogman seemed to have flippered his way across the chimney-piece and back again.

Joan, wearing a smile of quiet enjoyment, was stripping the dampened wallpaper away from the wall with a scraper, and inwardly hot with resentment. It was an old ploy of Cissie's, she was thinking, this exaggerated pleasure in the humdrum. Making drudgery divine was her speciality, since power often lies in the simple statement: 'I'm having a better time than you are.'

Cissie always has to enjoy herself the most, Joan thought, hacking viciously away at the drifting clouds she had so admired in 1938. Had she been of a different turn of mind, Joan might well have asked herself exactly why Cissie acted on this compulsion, and drawn some comforting conclusions from answering the question. But as it was Joan only felt annoyance at being presented with the same old gambit once again, coupled with an almost overmastering desire to try wallpaper wetting for herself, because it was obviously such fun.

Still, nothing, absolutely nothing, Joan told herself sternly, would make her ask Cissie to give her a try at it, because this would be exactly what Cissie wanted, and Joan was determined not to give it to her – for her own good, Joan reasoned. For her own good Cissie should be brought to realize that she fooled no one with her childish tricks.

Thus Joan had adopted the smile of quiet enjoyment, partly to convince her sister that she envied her the soapy washcloth not one whit, and partly to persuade her that wallpaper scraping was really glorious fun too, so that Cissie would eventually be forced to offer a swap.

'We're doing well, we are. A team, that's us,' said Cissie, looking about her. Two walls nearly done already, she thought gaily. Finish these two, then coffee all round.

The thought of the little extra treat of coffee made her lungs fill with the tight air of real fleeting happiness.

'Here, Joanie, want to swop?'

Daft Joanie, as usual, looked a bit dazed. Cissie waited kindly for the answer.

'Oh well, suppose we may as well.'

'Right, I'll put the kettle on, back in a sec,' called Cissie as she bounced into the passage.

Joan swished the cloth around in the bucket of water, which felt surprisingly cold, and straightened up cautiously.

The room looked familiar and yet terribly changed, as sick people look when they are taken to hospital. Joan threw the cloth, underarm and not very hard and then stood for a while, her arms at her sides, looking down at the floor where the sodden cloth had landed.

She thought of the last time this room had been re-papered, and wondered if her life in the intervening forty years would not have been quite different, possibly better, had she been firmer or more far-sighted or, in short, more like somebody else, when she was young.

Joan remembered painting the windowsills in 1938, with a bandage round her hand. For ten hours every weekday and five every Saturday morning she had sat before a sewing-machine, lining collars and wrist-bands for gentle-men's dressing-gowns. The morning after the decorating had started she had run the sewing-machine over the middle finger of her right hand, and broken the needle. No one could find the broken end, so on the way home from work she had called in at the hospital, where they had X-rayed her whole hand, and afterwards shown her the photograph, all lit up from behind; her own skeletal hand, with an inch of shining needle lying aslant amidst the shadowed flesh. Hadn't it been Cissie who'd told her that the piece of broken needle would move about her body like a slow-motion torpedo, aiming itself at her heart?

Nothing could have been different, thought Joan comfor-tingly. She remembered how it felt to be young; it was hardly different from the way she felt now, except that forty years before, there had been more possibilities to be afraid of.

'Right then, let's get this bit done, you okay? Where's that scraper, here it is, now then, whoops!'

Cissie carved a great arc out of the brown wet drifting clouds and stood back, in fencer's pose. 'Have at you!'

She danced forward, carved out a circle, nipped in eyes and mouth, and bounced backwards again.

'Coffee in five minutes!'

Joan, soaping and wetting, smiled at Cissie's invitation, and thought that Cissie would probably give her back the scraper after coffee. She saw herself making strange elegant cut-outs, so that everyone left their work and crowded round to exclaim and admire. Someone, Jessie perhaps or better still Gareth, would say seriously, 'D'you know, I think these show a real talent, a definite sense of style and movement,' or something like that. In the meantime Cissie must not suspect Joan wanted the scraper back, and so Joan put the smile of quiet enjoyment back on, and prepared herself to wait.

'Found a drawing in the passage, on the walls,' said Gareth over his mug of instant. Another week at the most, he reminded himself. Another week and they were sure to throw the old hag out.

'A Spitfire,' he went on aloud, 'in pencil.'

'Dropping bombs with stripes on 'em,' grinned Cissie, shaking her head. She'd been quite wrong about Gareth, she was thinking; he was really a very nice boy, coming here night after night and promising to stay all weekend too, and his eyes had really lit up when she'd told him how well Mum was doing this evening, sitting up and almost her old self again, nice blue eyes he had too, nothing like Jessie's, must have got them from his dad, and he'd been a good-looking chap too, though a bit on the small side and rather fat in the face for his size.

'That'd be Jimmy,' Jessie said.

'He used to drive us all mad –'

'On his school-books –'

'And hymnbook –'

'And submarines –'

'Always making pictures.'

'Mind you,' said Jessie with a little smile, 'it was always the *same* drawings.'

Cissie shot her a certain look.

'Surprising what you do find, decorating,' said Jeff heartily, having intercepted the look. They could hardly afford a row now, he thought, what with umpteen yards of wallpaper in ribbons all about. He remembered the postcard from Marion, and stealthily moved one hand down to the pocket of his overalls, to touch its pinked edge with his fingertips. He promised himself another quick look at it when he next went to the toilet, though already he knew its contents off by heart:

Dear Mum and Dad and all, arrived safely! at 9 o'clock, weather sunny, hotel fabulous, I tried the squid again tonight but Barry wouldn't, see you soon! Love, Marion and Barry.

And she'd be back at the end of next week, after all.

'You coloured the outhouse wall, that time, you remember? You and Jessie, Cis. You remember.'

'Ooh yes, with wax crayons! Every brick a different colour, remember, Cissie?' Jessie laughed and tutted. She was glad she'd kept on coming now, though at first things had been so uncomfortable, with everyone so tense and no one knowing where to start. It had been just like one of those plays, she thought, one of those incoherent television plays that you watched for a few minutes and then turned over, or went back to your knitting. But now it was more like a party, a lovely little party every evening, and Gareth making such a good impression on everyone and behaving just as if he were ordinary like everyone else.

Joan was remembering the crayoned outhouse. It was not a pleasant memory for her, but there was no fending it off now.

There was Cissie, hefty as a little pony, with hips to put her sarcastic fists on even at six years of age, and sly Jessie, scarcely a year younger, naughtily pretending not to know any better than Cissie, though always she had.

'What you done!' Herself, hoarse young Joan, aghast beside the outhouse. Each brick had been separately coloured in, each mottled dirty brick scribbled over in flakes and crescents of scarlet, green, purple, yellow, and orange. The outhouse vibrated with colour like a maddened chameleon.

'My God, Mum'll murder you! And look at you, look at the pair of you!' Cissie and Jessie were smeared almost as thickly as the outhouse, with an admix of streaky soot between the colours.

Joan remembered her own self, wearing a thin plait on either side of her face, and a blue dress long grown out of; she'd let the hem down herself, but the let-down bit was a darker blue than the rest, so you could see what she'd done.

First I was pleased because it was me that had caught them, not Mum. I thought I could show them I was on the grown-ups' side now, but still willing to help them out. I felt grown-up when I caught them. But they didn't care, they just grinned at their boots and at one another, and they didn't care at all.

'You wait then, I'll tell her myself this minute!'

And I run down the path, there's Mum in the kitchen.

'You'll never guess what them kids've done now!'

I followed her back up the path outside. She'd been irritated with me, dragging her out. I was trembling. She was wearing a tight new skirt, cut very short. I saw the back of her legs, and that skirt swing, and I was scared.

Then she saw what they'd done. She stood still for a second, staring. She unfolded her arms. She gave a sort of whooping noise, and she roared, she roared laughing. She rubbed the kids' heads, one under each hand, curly heads, both of them.

'Oh, it's lovely! Ha, ha! Lovely!' and she laughed and

laughed. 'Wool, the bloody thing couldn't look much worse, could it!'

She had given each little girl a kiss, and Jessie had swung her head sideways, to give me a certain clear look . . .

And me –

Modern Joan, sitting on the sofa between Jeff and Cissie, felt her throat tighten with anguish so that she was jerked back into the present by the click in her own breathing.

I knew that if it had been me, me at their age doing that, I'd have got a hiding for it. A good hiding. And I felt so sad, so sad, I couldn't hardly speak any more that day, nor the next.

Completely out of it, Gareth was thinking. What on earth could she be thinking about? He was reminded of schizophrenics conversing with the invisible; and of watching someone else make a telephone call: the little smiles, the ingratiating eyebrows, all as reflexive as a blink.

Do I do it? he wondered suddenly. Do I do it myself? It was a worrying idea. How would you be able to tell, unless someone watched you at it, and told you? Perhaps if you twisted your face about really severely you eventually felt the pulling strain of it. Though in that case Aunt Joan ought to have felt what she was up to just now. And I saw her at it, and would I tell her?

Excuse me, Aunt Joan, d'you realize you're making lots of funny faces sitting there all lost in thought?

No, no, no, thought Gareth. I'll just have to keep a sort of watch on myself for a while, be on the safe side, make sure my thoughts are for internal use only.

This last phrase cheered him up so much, however, that he presently rejoined the general conversation, and forgot to check up on his features at all.

TWELVE

'SHE said she didn't want to be cremated. Just come out with it.'

'I've always been afraid of fire,' returned Cissie dramatically. A few icing-sugar streaks of paper still smeared the walls.

'See that crack.'

'It's an old one. Or it'd've torn the paper, see?'

'You know that Dierdre. You know, that, you know, friend of mine?'

'Oh yes.' Cissie edged at a crescent smear of paper with small and concentrated movements. Removing the last obstinate trace of wallpaper without pulling off too much of the old soft plaster beneath was a delicate operation, Cissie had discovered. Delicate but satisfying, and on the whole very like scab-picking, which involved similar tantalizing possibilities of removing more than was at first intended.

'Anyway, Dierdre,' said Joan importantly. 'She told me. You listening, Cis?' Joan had remembered Dierdre's strange story late the night before, as she had waited for sleep, and had at once pictured Cissie's wonder and amazement as she, Joan, related it to her. It was true that the story

102

made Dierdre appear even more of an oddity than Cissie at present thought her, but by passing on her friend's secret Joan felt that she would be siding herself with Cissie and normality against Dierdre's strangeness, rather than ranging herself at Dierdre's side, as she would undoubtedly do, she had reasoned during the night, by keeping the story to herself.

And Cissie would understand that she was being cast as normality, that Joan was paying her the deepest of compliments as well as entertaining her: being gossiped to can be an act of flattery quite as sincere as imitation.

Accordingly, with some excitement, Joan began: 'Anyway, Dierdre. She told me. You listening, Cis?'

' 'Course,' said Cissie, her nose almost touching the wall.

'Dierdre's father, he died. Just when Princess Anne got married, when was that?'

'Seventy-three, wasn't it? Or seventy-four. I dunno.'

'Wool, anyway. He'd wanted to be cremated, not like Mum, he wanted to be cremated. He used to work for the Co-op. So Dierdre had him cremated. And afterwards they give her this urn, with his ashes in, you know like they do. A cream plaster urn.'

'Oh yes.'

'Dierdre's brother, he works up North, he says to Dierdre, Here you give me that. He wants to keep it on the mantelpiece.'

Cissie made a mild noise to indicate disgust. She was thinking of a story she would tell Joan when Joan had finished, and beginning to feel slightly impatient. Hers was sure to be the better story, too.

'Anyway Dierdre says, No way! No way. Because she'd lived with her dad all these years and nursed him through his final illness. No way are you getting these ashes, says Dierdre. To her brother. And he goes mad, they have this terrible row about it right there in the crematorium with the man still there. But you'll never guess what they did in the end!'

'No I wouldn't,' agreed Cissie tersely.

'Wait a minute, listen. They take the urn home. Dierdre lays out some paper on the kitchen table. Christmas wrapping paper it was, with little pink pine-trees. She puts it picture-side down. And they pour out her dad, his ashes, onto the paper, into a pile, and they divide them up into two equal halves, and the brother takes one and Dierdre takes one!'

Cissie straightened up and turned round.

'Yes, Dierdre said to me at the finish that she'd scattered her share of the ashes down the back garden, she's on the ground floor see, she scattered the ashes down the back garden, and when it's raining, she thinks to herself, Poor old Dad out there in the wet, and then she thinks, Oh no it's not, it's half of him out there in the wet.'

Cissie let out a sharp gasp of laughter.

'And then she says, Dierdre says,' Joan continued excitedly, 'when you visit a grave you should be all reverent and that, and thinking of the person when he was alive and how good he was and so on, but I can't, she says, I go past the bit of ground where he is, and I can't help it, I think to myself, wool, which bit of him is it?'

'Oh-my-God,' laughed Cissy squeamishly. Pink with triumph, Joan laughed too.

'Which bit of him is it?' Joan repeated in Dierdre's deep hopeless tones.

'Oh don't, oh, it's terrible,' cried Cissie. 'Oh, she was pulling your leg!'

'Oh no, I don't think so,' said Joan, suddenly sober. 'What'd she do a thing like that for?' And she remembered promising Dierdre never to pass the story on to another living soul.

'His final resting places!' shouted Cissie hilariously.

Joan laughed with her. An image of Dierdre's earnest St

Bernard face, imploring silence, arose in her mind. Get lost, she told the image impenitently. You shouldn't go around telling people such things if you don't want them spread about.

'Whenever I see her now,' cried Joan recklessly, 'whenever I see her now, I think, wool, here's the woman who buried half her father!'

Over a lunch of ham salad prepared by Jessie, Cissie retold and expertly embroidered Dierdre's story, thus elevating it to family-legend status. Now all Lily's descendants, unto the third and fourth generations, would sooner or later come to know of the Women Who Buried Half Her Father, as they knew the old tales of Lily and the half-pound of best butter, of the reluctant crab-boiler's revenge, or the thrilling history of the wild-eyed gent in Victoria Park, who was encountered by Lily's mother late one dismal gas-lit evening, and who had made certain advances, which Lily's mother had indignantly (so she said afterwards) rejected, though at the time she had had no inkling of his identity: only after sifting the evidence for upwards of five years had Lily's mother realized just who the wild-eyed gent must have been, thus herself becoming, to a wide circle of family and friends, the Woman Who Escaped Jack the Ripper.

All Lily's grandchildren know the story of the Woman Who Escaped Jack the Ripper; some of them even believe it.

'Fighting for the urn,' declaimed Cissie over her ham-and-Branston. 'She grabs it, he grabs it off of her –'

'Half a tombstone –'

'Here lieth half the remains –' put in Gareth.

'But she must be so peculiar, Joan,' wailed Jessie, imagining how smartly she would switch channels on Dierdre if Dierdre were a new television play.

'Oh, she's all right otherwise,' said Joan faintly, weakened with remorse. She had realized that Cissie would undoubt-edly signal her knowledge of the story to Dierdre when next they met: she would make some chortling allusion to fractions, or urns, or Christmas wrapping paper, and Dierdre would know she was betrayed, and turn a gaze of canine malignity upon her friend, who quailed over her lettuce at the very idea.

Don't tell her I told you! she imagined herself begging Cissie as she had on many other occasions in the past. As Cissie's response to this plea in the past had merely been to spill the beans earlier rather than later, Joan knew her position was a hopeless one.

'It's a terrible thing, children doing that to their parents,' said Jeff abruptly, breaking his long silence. All this laugh-ing over death, he had thought disgustedly, and the poor old bag still in the hospital. 'It's not right,' he added aloud.

'Oh you –' began Cissie crossly at this piece of wet-blanketry. 'Oh you –' she broke off, noticing his lemony pallor and remembering his weak stomach and the ulcers that, according to the doctors, came and went with the mysterious irregularity of a mushroom-ring.

'Zit playing you up again?' she inquired tenderly.

'I'm all right, I'm all right,' said Jeff hastily.

'He has such trouble with his stomach,' Cissie informed the company brightly. 'Anybody want any more ham?' She was determined to keep up the party atmosphere. Paintwork next, miles of it; a long afternoon ahead unless you could get some fun out of it.

'Gareth? You have a bit more, growing lad like you.'

'I'm only growing sideways these days,' returned Gareth, rising to the occasion. Cissie roared.

'You ought to hear some of the things he tells me,' said Jessie proudly, 'enough to make you feel ill, some of them.'

'Hospital things,' said Jeff apprehensively. Unaccount-ably his lower ribs seemed to have grown a size too small for him over the last half-hour. Furtively, pulling out his shirt at the front to conceal movements beneath its overhang, he undid the top button of his trousers.

'Tea all round?' asked Joan, ceremonially carrying in from the kitchen the big old family teapot. This was one of the great moments she had earlier envisaged but, still worrying hard about Dierdre, she forgot to savour it properly and by the time she realized what she had missed the teas were all poured. It's too late to enjoy it now, she told herself over the family chorus of tinkling teaspoons. Since she had realized that Dierdre would inevitably discover her treachery, Joan had felt abjectly guilty and traitorous.

Too late to enjoy it now, she told herself, and, she added spitefully, it just serves you right.

Jeff sipped his tea cautiously and, after making sure that he was unobserved, took a good long look at his nephew Gareth's hands. Since Jeff's two boys, staggering, or so they had both implied, beneath a deadly weight of sorrow and remorse, had gone to an away match at Coventry, Jeff and Gareth had worked together all morning, stripping away the stairwell's ancient sepia roses in friendly silence.

A pleasant enough youngster, Gareth had seemed to his uncle; a little on the cocky side, perhaps, but pleasant enough. Jeff had forgotten how Gareth earned his living. How else, Jeff wondered now, did Gareth use those scrubbed nail-bitten fingers of his? Where else had those fingers been?

There he sat, not two feet away, a young chap who had delved about in other people's moving wet insides, who had touched their butcher's shop innards with those very same fingers. Did he think of such things as work? Jeff asked himself with something between awe and disgust. Had he seen babies born, and looked upon birth as simply another crust honestly earned?

And if he had, wasn't that rather a loss for a young chap? For an instant Jeff sat in his own kitchen in 1958, and gazed with blessed love into his immortal baby's eyes. Would he have felt that, the love that had given him so much painful happiness, if he'd seen other people's babies born and thought of it all as a job?

Jeff took another, sharper glance at his nephew. It was almost enough to make you pity the lad, Jeff thought to himself: everything in life would seem secondhand to him, Birth, Suffering, Death. All those important things. There would be little for him to wonder over, when the time came. And he would grow accustomed to seeing the horrors of life descend upon the heads of other people; it would be doubly hard on him when they descended at last upon his own.

Gareth meanwhile was considering which of his own repertoire of grotesqueries might equal the Woman Who Buried Half Her Father. The Brain Tumour Man was clearly a little too technical for present company, and the Woman with the Sore Finger far too close to home. Was the history of the Man From China simply too revolting?

'Joanie used to bring home some shocking stories from that hospital,' said Cissie cosily. 'Things that went on in the old days. You remember that Girl Who Had a Boil, Joanie? Scared the living daylights out of me, that did.'

'Could tell you about a Man From China,' said Gareth, by now quite anxious to excel.

'Oh, no, not that one, not that one!' cried Jessie with alarmed delight, and careful to let everyone know that she had heard the story before. 'That's too awful!'

'It's got a happy ending,' said Gareth smiling.

'Go on, go on then,' urged Cissie, leaning across the table.

'Right. This is a true story, I read it in one of the medical journals. So I think it's true anyway. It concerns a Man From China. Who was born, poor chap, with an accessory head.'

'A what?' asked Jeff, lowering his teacup.

'Extra head,' Jessie nodded at him.

'My Gawd,' breathed Cissie, leaning back in her chair.

'Yes, an accessory head. It was on his face. Just a little head.' Gareth tapped his right cheekbone. 'Just about here, it was, a little head with hair and eyes and eyelashes. It had a bit of a brain, not much, but a little, and a mouth, with teeth. Whenever the Man ate something, the accessory head dribbled.'

Cissie snickered with horror.

'Anyway the Man was thirty-five years old before the extra head was kindly removed by someone or other. An operation. At the end of the article it said that the Man was very happy to be alone at last but was considering getting married. Presumably no one'd take him on before. Three being a crowd.'

Looking round the little circle of faces at this climax Gareth saw at once that the story had after all been a bad choice. Too late he saw that the best stories are about human foibles, and not about God's. And the stories which allow hearers to say to themselves, 'I'd have acted differently, I'd have done better than that,' are the stories people like to hear most of all, thought Gareth.

'Is this the sort of thing you lot always talk about over your dinner?' demanded Jeff. His gaze across the table held some meaning Gareth could not interpret.

'If that's the sort of thing you hear all day, my lad, I'm surprised you can keep your dinner down,' said Cissie roundly. She stood up to collect the plates, and the meal was over.

Gareth quickly swallowed the cooling tea left in his cup. All I did was disgust them, he thought, and as it was a God-foible story they had no one to focus their disgust on but me. And after all they are only laity, and particularly unsophisticated laity at that. One week more, that's all I'm going to take. One week more. Of this bunch.

Still, irritatingly enough, he felt he had rather disgraced himself. He carried his teacup and saucer out to the kitchen to make some amends to Aunt Cissie, who was washing up.

Imagine it salivating though, whenever you ate. Imagine dabbing at its little mouth with your napkin. God. The things some people put up with, thought Gareth.

THIRTEEN

'SO who've you got? Lead me to her, do your worst.'

'Worst, eh? Well, you could have Bed Twenty-eight, I suppose. Since you're feeling brave.'

'Sometimes,' admitted Elizabeth, 'I think it would be quicker to ask them what they *don't* have wrong with them.'

'Bed Twenty-eight's not so bad as far as that goes. She's got a temper, though. And the language! Make a young thing like you blush. And last night she bit an aux.'

'She what?'

'Bit an aux. An auxiliary. Auxiliary nurse, yes?'

'Oh,' Elizabeth giggled uneasily.

'Said afterwards she was all confused, "Everything went black, Doctor," you know the sort of thing. But she's no more confused than I am at the moment, she just felt like biting someone if you ask me.'

'Know how she feels,' said Elizabeth.

'Don't we all,' returned the nurse instantly. 'But seriously, you know, she's a very difficult patient.'

'Good practice.'

'Well, enjoy yourself. We'll be at tea in Sister's office. If we hear the sounds of a struggle –'

'Wailings and gnashings of teeth,' said Elizabeth.

'We'll come and haul her off you.'

'You're really supportive, you know that?'

'We try to please.' The nurse grinned and disappeared into an ante-room.

Elizabeth drew, consciously, a deep breath, held it for a count of three and slowly exhaled. I am perfectly calm, she told herself. I will forget nothing. I am perfectly calm.

She started off down the ward, the patient's notes under her arm, and a quite different mental voice, the small whine of defeat, whispered consolingly that this was all just for practice anyway, and so need not be taken too seriously. Shut up, thought Elizabeth sternly to this defeated whine, shut up! And she arrived beside Bed Twenty-eight wearing a heavy scowl of inner struggle.

'Hallo there,' smiled Elizabeth, unconsciously making an enormous and abrupt change of expression.

The patient, a plump but bruised-looking ancient, made a distinct start of alarm.

Elizabeth sat down beside the bed.

'I've just come to ask you a few questions, if you don't mind.'

'Ain't got much choice, have I,' said the ancient unexpectedly. 'Fuckin' hospitals.'

'Ah, you could say no, you know.'

'Fat lot a good that'd do me. No,' the ancient went on gloomily, 'I should let you all learn off of me. Nothing else I'm good for.'

'Oh, no, not really,' smiled Elizabeth weakly.

There was a short pause, while the ancient turned her eyes upon Elizabeth with antique deliberation, and looked at her. Elizabeth was reminded instantly of a monkey she had once seen in a zoo. The monkey had sat very still in one corner of its cage, forlorn resignation in every curve of its small body, while all the time its quick human eyes seemed to rove the crowd of onlookers with an intimate, insider's contempt. The monkey's eyes had met Elizabeth's and in them she had seen a sort of coaxing jeer, such as, she had imagined, the desperate Czechs might have worn, as they poked flowers into the gunbarrels of Russian tanks: the jeer of hopelessness ranged against omnipotence.

Something of this in the patient's small old eyes hit Elizabeth rather hard as she picked up her clipboard from the bedside locker and began taking the history.

'First of all, please, why are you in hospital at the moment?'

'What, don't you know?'

'Ah ...' Elizabeth decided, rashly perhaps, on the woman-to-woman approach. 'I need to find out, d'you see, whether *you* know exactly why you're here.'

''Course I know. What you bleeding take me for?' asked the patient indignantly.

'Oh, you'd be surprised, Mrs Lorrigan, at the number of people who aren't really sure, not in their own words.'

'Wouldn't surprise me at all.'

'Right then, perhaps you could tell me –'

'You're a student, ain't you? There you are then. I ain't telling you what's wrong with me. That's for you to find out, innit.'

'Mrs Lorrigan, I *know* what's wrong with you –'

'Well then,' shouted Lily triumphantly, 'what the bleeding hell d'you keep asking me for?'

FOURTEEN

AT the top of the stairwell Gareth was coming to the last
of the sepia roses. They had been mildly irritating him all
morning. There was something facetious about them, he
felt, something vaguely Disneyfied, as if at any moment
they might roll sepia eyes and sing in close American
harmony.

With aggressive relish he scored a wide swathe through
the last of the roses' yellowed panels, and then stopped
short, electrified by that half-heard, half-felt sensation, that
faint purring *crunch* along the nerves, which proceeds from
sudden sharp surprise.

Set in the cracked plaster in front of him, laid bare for
the first time in God knew how many years, was the painted
edge of a little wooden door. A secret cupboard, flush with
the wall! A secret cupboard papered over and forgotten!
Gareth uttered a single squeak of excited delight. What
might lie behind that secret door? What had lain waiting
for release throughout the decades?

Treasure? The fat little casket, overflowing with doub-
loons and ropes of pearls; or the flat black tin crackling with
important documents, deeds, hidden wills, all-important

codicils, negotiable bonds; or a bar of solid gleaming gold, stamped with the Russian Imperial eagle?

Gareth, calming down, attended properly to these theatrical suggestions and actually sniggered aloud. It was like archaeology, he thought gaily, as he stripped away the rest of the paper over the cupboard door: tap the right stratum of the most well-ordered mind, and you'd still lay bare a thick deposit of second-hand images, the fossil remains of a hundred adventure stories for boys.

Still, he thought, as he peeled away the last of the singing sepia roses, someone had clearly gone to the trouble of slapping paint around the edges of the door, to gum it to the plaster. Why would anyone take trouble to deprive themselves of cupboard space? Perhaps it had been for fashion; part of the drive to force elderly buildings into modern dress, like knocking cosy little rooms into open-plan.

Lily would have had no appreciation of the sort of architectural oddity that makes a house individual. Not she. Such appreciation was, Gareth thought, inspecting his own responses, a function of middle-classness.

'Hallo, what you got there?' Gareth turned. It was Uncle Jeff, halfway up the last flight of stairs, his ankles curled about with ribbons of sepia roses. He kicked out at them amiably.

'Come and see.'

Jeff danced his way up the stairs.

'Get off, blast you. Oh. A cupboard.' He peered at it, stiffly bending forwards from the waist, his hands in his trouser-pockets. After a few moments' close inspection he straightened up again.

''S funny.'

'Yes.'

'Anything in it?' asked Jeff after another pause.

'I haven't tried to open it yet.'

'Paint round the edges,' Jeff pointed out.

'Yes.'

'Are you going to –'

'I don't see why not,' said Gareth.

'Here,' said Jeff, suddenly energetic, 'let me have a go.' He produced a wallpaper scraper and deliberately inserted the tip of it between wood and plaster, breaking the line of reddish-brown paint someone long ago had taken the trouble to slap down. Carefully Jeff ran the scraper round the cupboard's edges, with a gentle sawing motion that made Gareth think of his mother Jessie in her kitchen, loosening a new cake from its tin with a blunt knife. Thinking of her, he began, for the first time since finding the cupboard, to feel a little frightened. Perhaps Jessie knew why the cupboard had been hidden. Perhaps she knew whether anything lay inside. Perhaps she knew exactly what the anything was. And perhaps the cupboard would be better left alone, sealed and forgotten.

Noticing this anxious turn of his own thoughts, Gareth realized all at once that Jeff was taking a ridiculously long time about breaking the cupboard's paint-seal. No doubt he was the sort of person who habitually opened his Christmas presents very slowly and carefully, in order to preserve the paper and ribbon for next year, by which time they'd always been lost anyway, thought Gareth, by now quite outraged with impatience.

'Here,' he said abruptly, 'it's my turn.' With clenched teeth he forced his paper-scraper along the door's edge, peeling away a long splinter of gleaming, bone-coloured wood along with a dozen tiny corkscrews of reddish-brown paint, which sprang away from the crack to litter themselves among the fallen roses at his feet.

'Now lean on it, lean on it,' advised Jeff without excitement, tapping his wallpaper scraper gently against his lips. 'Lean on it.'

Gareth wordlessly jammed his scraper as far into the cupboard's edge as it would go, and heaved against it sideways. The metal edge of it bit painfully into his palms.

'Door's cracking,' said Jeff helpfully. 'Put it up the top, work it round.'

Gareth poked the scraper in along the top edge and hung his own weight from it.

'Come on,' he grunted, 'come-on-you-bastard-thing.'

'Now the bottom, it's coming.'

Gareth squeezed the scraper in lower down, and pushed up onto its handle.

'It's coming,' advised Jeff, with a faint colour of excitement in his voice.

'Come-on-you!'

'Nearly!'

'Hah!'

The door gave a sharp dry creak and pushed itself out on its hinges.

'Gotcha!'

Gareth dropped the scraper and bent his fingers over the protruding edge.

'It's tight.'

He pulled fiercely, and his damp fingertips slid off the wood with painful abruptness.

'Ow!'

'Here.' Like a pianist feeling his way into a complicated chord Jeff carefully splayed his own fingers out on the door's edge, and, after a great deal of peering along its entire length to make sure everything was correctly in position, gave his wrists a sharp judicious jerk.

The door swung open.

Oh Jesus, thought Gareth bleakly. With pounding heart he laid his hand on the little door and pulled it wide open so that he could see into the dark space behind it.

'Uh.' Jeff made an uneasy snorting noise.

Lying on the floor of the cupboard was a large shapeless greeny-gold cloth bundle, tied about with string.

There was nothing else, not even a shelf.

Gingerly Gareth reached in a hand and pressed the bundle with one reluctant finger. It gave off a faint powdery crackling sound, as of ancient paper beneath the outer wrap of material.

'What d'you reckon?' asked Jeff, on a whisper.

'Open it?'

'Not – down there?' Jeff gestured with one hand, to indicate the lower floors where his wife was somewhere plying sandpaper and, judging by the indignant noises rising even up here, to the third level, innocently listening to *Any Questions*.

Gareth thought of Jessie, and of her limited level of sophistication.

'No, up here. We could go in there,' and he pointed at one of the empty rooms behind them.

'And open it.'

Jeff nodded. 'All right.'

Gareth started towards the nearest door. Jeff stayed where he was, mute beside the cupboard.

'What's the matter?'

'Here.' Jeff pointed at the bundle, still inside the cupboard. 'Here.' He swallowed. 'You carry it.'

'You don't think it'll be too much of a shock? I mean, suppose she liked it the way it was?'

'Wool,' said Cissie exasperatedly, 'it's no good talking like that now, is it, wool, is it?'

Joan shook her head.

'Right. She'll love it anyway. She'll love it. Now you get going on that door and I'll do this one and we'll work our way towards each other, all right?'

Joan wrapped her square of sandpaper around the wooden block Jeff had given her that morning and began resignedly to fret at the living-room door with it. She felt unusually grumpy with Cissie this afternoon, because Cissie, bringing the radio in from the kitchen, had noticed the small incrustation of raw pastry on the volume dial, held there unchanged since Joan had turned up the Archers in the middle of a jam tart several years before.

Cissie had scratched the volume dial clean, at which Joan had felt greatly offended. In Cissie's place Joan would have pretended not to notice the pastry at all. It was downright rude of Cissie, she thought, to go about cleaning up other people's property without so much as a by-your-leave.

Joan sighed, scraping dully away at her door. It was other people's filth, perhaps, that annoyed; other people's, not your own. Bet Cissie's got cake-mix all over her radio and never bothered about it, Joan thought, smiling widely at the thought. I wonder why that bit of old pastry never bothered me at all, though, when I saw it every day for years?

All that cleaning during the War, maybe. Floors, bed-pans, gallipots, syringes, lockers, windowsills, curtain rails, bedsteads, saucepans, china, splints and drip-stands. Scrub-a-dub-dub. Yes Sister, sorry Sister, right away, Sister. Bossy old besoms: Sister French with her long gleaming face and bony hands, on her knees conducting quiet, threatening prayers amongst the staff at shift-changes; fat Sister Burwash, mad as a March hare, buoyantly jaunty as a balloon in a starched apron, who'd finally had a stroke on the floor of her office, sensible lace-ups pointing up at the ceiling from behind her own desk. And a staff nurse Joan had once been quite friendly with, on Chesterfield ward: Jewish; what was her name?

Horowitz. Very foreign, that was it, thought Joan, still having at the living-room door. Horowitz.

'Coming to the flicks, Lorrigan? I'm bored to death.'

And suddenly Joan was sitting in the warm cinema twilight with a small Scottish sergeant, watching Bette Davis losing Humphrey Bogart. The sergeant had tried to hold Joan's hand earlier, but not very insistently, so Joan so far had no regrets about agreeing to his company. Joan had often gone to the pictures all alone in those days, since her sisters were all grown up and courting. That was lonely: no one to whisper with during the dull bits, or clutch at during the exciting ones. All you could do when the film flagged and you came to yourself was look about at the shadowed heads all around, at their mildly risible variations in size and shape and height, or up at the smoke curling through the angled moving lights of projection.

But the worst part of solitary cinema-going was the interval, when the lights came up and the organist began: when everyone else could see you were alone, and everyone else in twos or threes, or laughing, singing bunches. You had to smile then, and pretend that you were having a good time sitting there by yourself.

Not tonight though, not this particular night, with the small alien sergeant by her side. When the lights went up the world would see a man beside her. And sitting down no one would realize that he was no taller than she. In present and anticipated happiness Joan had surrendered herself to the hands of Hollywood.

The Scottish sergeant had glanced at her from time to time during the film, little darting sideways glances. Was he, perhaps, admiring her looks? Joan wondered, when she noticed what he was doing; and if he wasn't, if he didn't, why had he asked her out in the first place? She was sure he knew; men always knew exactly what they were doing. And why, and what they were saying, and why they said it.

Whereas she, Joan, often had no idea why she behaved and spoke as she did, which made it doubly hard for her to guess what lay behind the communications of others. Especially of men, determined, certain, mysterious men.

During the interval the sergeant had got up straight away and gone to get ice-creams. Joan had smiled and waved at him as he stood in the queue so that people nearby would know that she was not alone.

'You enjoyed that, then,' he said, as he sat down beside her.

'Ooh, thanks ever so much. Yes, I did, it was smashing.'

'Thought you liked it. You were pulling your wee faces all the time.'

'What?'

'Well away, you were,' grinned the Scottish sergeant, taking a pull at his ice-cream. 'When Bette's all sorrowful, so were you, when Bogey bares his teeth, so did you! When her sister gets kilt you should have seen yer face!'

He laughed and guyed her, popping his eyes and gaping his mouth in mock horror.

'Oh no . . . did I?' asked Joan, trying to smile.

'Och, don't look like that! It's just my fun, that's all. You carry on enjoying yourself, hen.' And he patted her knee quite hard.

Present Joan, still sanding the door, remembered how long the second feature and the news had lasted, how she had sat stone-faced throughout the trailers, turned at the end and said, Thank you so much but that she would see herself home, thanks, and gone straight back to her tiny room at the nurses' home shaking with relief. Horowitz, even dopey Horowitz, had noticed something was wrong when she popped in for cocoa later that evening.

'Here, Lorrigan, he didn't jump you, did he?'

Supposing he hadn't said what he said, thought present Joan, what might have happened? Or supposing he had – and gone on saying things like it too, because that's the sort of thing men say – but supposing I hadn't minded? Supposing that was the sort of thing everyone else put up with, so that they could get married?

Perhaps that was what being attractive to men was all about, thought Joan: it was not minding what they said.

I was too idealistic, thought Joan, reaching the conclusion

which usually lay waiting at the end of these familiar tracks. Too idealistic, too –

'Joanie!' A long wail from Cissie. 'Look what you're doing!'

Joan looked down with surprise at the door. She had rubbed a largish patch of paint clean off, baring the wood.

'Ooh, sorry, Cis, I wasn't thinking.'

Cissie looked briefly up at the ceiling, slowly shaking her head.

'Just the surface, all right, so the new paint sticks. Just a scratch. Okay?'

Joan nodded, abashed.

'Never mind, it'll cover. Just get on with it, right?' Honestly, Cissie thought sighingly, it was like being with a little kid, you couldn't hardly look away. 'And try to concentrate for once, see?'

'Come on. Quick, before someone comes up.'

'Shut the door.'

'Nah, leave it ajar – looks less, you know, as if something's going on.'

Turning from the door Jeff realized that the room he had chosen was that very same empty top-floor room he had spent one sleepless night in, on a turn-up bedstead in 1945, the night before Cissie and he had tied the knot.

'You know,' said Gareth, glancing round, 'if this place was in Knightsbridge it'd be worth a fortune.' He was panting a little. He had not drawn breath while the bundle was in his arms. It was very light. Something within it, something deeply padded in many layers of something else, had softly butted to and fro with each step.

There had been a rocking-horse beneath the window, Jeff remembered, a battered brown-spotted creature, with flared wooden nostrils and reins pale and velvety with age and a yellowed scrub of horsehair tail. Straddling it Jeff had slowly, carefully, lowered himself until he was sure it would take his weight, which wasn't so much in those days, and he had rocked himself and the little horse slowly back and forth, so gently that the floorboards had stayed silent beneath him. The toes of his great army boots, Jeff remembered, had just fitted into the small iron stirrups.

'Worth a fortune.'

'Beg pardon?' asked Jeff.

'Nothing, nothing.' Gareth was thinking that he would like a nice sterile pair of surgical gloves on, to protect his own skin from whatever lay within the bundle at his feet. I've hit the stratum of Hammer Horror, he thought, recognizing the fossils of a hundred X films all pressing about him as he put out a hand to snap the bundle's ancient strings. I can stand anything so long as it isn't *wet*, he thought dismally.

'All right?' prompted Jeff anxiously. He would have liked to tell the boy to get a move on, since they could hardly stand here funking it all afternoon, but saw that if he did so Gareth might well seize the opportunity to rise angrily and say, 'All right then, you open it!' Which was the last thing Jeff wanted.

'All right?'

Gareth shrugged and broke the string easily with one hand, and pulled up the outer edge of cloth, very gingerly, as if he expected an explosion. Laying it flat upon the floor he saw that the cloth had been wrapped pattern-side in, as now he could make out its faint design of green and yellow shells. Three more folds to straighten. One. Two. Three. The last edge was sewn irregularly with blackened metal rings.

'It's brocade,' said Gareth, touching a yellow shell with one finger, feeling the smooth damp-dry slide of silk.

'It's a curtain,' said Jeff, crouched down opposite his nephew.

Gareth sat back on his heels. Lying squarely in the middle

of the cloth, the oblong newspaper-wrapped bundle seemed to him to have a sinisterly obvious shape.

'I think I know what it is,' he whispered, and felt, from the coldness of his lips, that his face had whitened.

'What then'

Gareth shook his head. Hammer Horror stratum, he told himself resolutely. Second-hand images. Don't be fooled by them. It's probably nothing but a poor people's treasure, paste jewellery, baby-curls, old Valentines, postcards, or cheap old china, ashtrays painted with A Present from Margate and actually worth something these days.

The newspaper was brittle, powdery to the touch.

'What's the date,' asked Jeff, stretching his head backwards and squinting down his nose, 'I can't see a thing without my glasses.'

'Um, September. The ninth. 1926.'

'Long time ago.'

'Yes.' Something big had happened in 1926, thought Gareth, who had never included History as one of his strong points. Something big. Was it a war? No, surely not. Something big had happened though, while here in Dunnett Street someone had wrapped and hidden something really rather small.

'When did they move here, you know, the family?' *Her* family, cravenly added Jeff to himself. Cissie's family, not mine.

'How should I know?'

Another layer of newspaper revealed itself, and another.

'Hmm.'

Beneath the last layer was a small green enamel box.

'Locked?'

Gareth pulled up on the lid. 'Yup.'

'Here. Use this.' Jeff handed over his paper-scraper.

Breathing noisily Gareth slid the top of the scraper between the box and lid and leant on it gently. A small litter of rust particles fell onto the floorboards with a light sparkling sound.

'Try the sides.'

Gareth complied. The box-lid shifted, came free.

Gareth drew a deep breath. He could feel his heart pounding in his throat, as if he had been running up a mountain.

Inside, more cloth; white cotton, peaked here and there into the stiffness of a dried-out stain. The stains had golden curlicued edges, like scalloped embroidery. The material crumbled and tore in his fingers as if it were tissue paper.

'My God,' cried Jeff, his fingers at his mouth.

'Jesus Christ,' whispered Gareth, starting back.

Inside, revealed, a little collapsed figure, a waxen image, unquestionably a human child, tucked into its enamel coffin as cosily as new shoes in a shoebox.

For several moments simple shock kept Jeff's eyes tightly closed. Then he was seized with a sudden dread that whatever lay in the box might, now that the lid of its coffin was opened, be able to sidle itself out onto the floorboards and somehow work its little pleated-parchment self closer and closer, until it could reach out its skeletal hand and touch him as he sat blinded behind his own eyelids.

This thought zipped Jeff's eyes open, propelled him forward on hands and knees, and poked out his right hand just far enough to slap the box-lid shut, and all before Jeff had consciously recovered from his surprise long enough to consider any movement at all.

Behind his hands Gareth was shaking with silent laughter. He peeped his scarlet face out from behind his fingers as Jeff crawled forwards, met his uncle's eyes and, like a giggly child meeting the eyes of its little fellow-giggler, burst into fresh paroxysms of hilarity.

'Here, you stop that,' ordered Jeff, contriving to whisper

from behind his own clenched teeth, 'you hysterical or what?'

Gareth gasped soberly, knuckled his wet eyes, bit his lower lip and, giving up the effort, lay on his back and giggled weakly at the ceiling.

'I was thinking,' he sobbed between seizures, 'you know, talk about heh heh heh, talk about skeletons in cupboards oh God ha ha ha –'

'You're hysterical!' hissed Jeff spitefully, but grinning all the same. 'Stop that! We got to think what to do.'

'Do?' Gareth sat up tremblingly. He felt that at any moment he might break into loud doleful tears.

'We go to the police,' he said, wiping his mouth with his sleeve. He sniffed damply. 'That's what we do.'

Jeff sat back, considering. 'It was real, right?'

Gareth sighed. 'Of course it's real.'

'And been there since 1926, right?'

'I suppose,' said Gareth sulkily. Do your bit for your bleeding bloody sodding horrible old relatives, he was thinking, and what happens, eh, what happens?

'Wool I don't see bringing the cops in. Why should we? It's none a their business.'

'What are you – it's a corpse, for Christ's sake! A body! What are we going to do with it? We've got to go to the police. We've got to do something with it,' hissed Gareth furiously.

'Don't see why,' said Jeff with a touch of that dogged obstinacy he usually resorted to when challenged by Cissie.

'You're crazy,' said Gareth flatly. 'How d'you suppose it got there? It didn't walk there, did it! Look at it!' He pushed the box-lid open again. There it lay, neatly flexed, its papery little limbs folded as if for birth. 'Look at it! It was murdered! Poor little sod,' he added, seeing its small drawn-up knees. 'Murdered,' he repeated.

'Not necessarily,' said Jeff stolidly, after a wince. Gareth was young, he was thinking; he's siding with the baby, that's what he's doing. He's got no children, so he still sides with the children. But me, I'm a father, a grandfather, and I can see both sides.

'Not necessarily. Maybe they couldn't afford to give it a proper burial. That sort of thing happened then. You don't know.'

So intent were they, so loud was their interchange of hisses, that neither Jeff nor Gareth heard footsteps on the stairs below, or even noticed the door swinging wide open until Joan was quite in the room with them. When she saw what lay on the floor between them she gave a little jump into the air.

'Oh.' She still had one hand on the doorknob. 'I see you found it then,' she said.

Joan, scrubbing her chastened way along the wainscoting towards Cissie, began after a few feet to grow exceedingly bored. *Any Questions* was by now entirely monopolizing Cissie's conversation, and besides it was putting her into a furious temper. ('Oh get lost!' Cissie had scornfully ordered a particularly soft-spoken bishop, who had asked her to really consider the feelings of Asian Immigrant women. 'What about my feelings,' she had asked him belligerently. 'What about them, eh? You old fool!' But the bishop had gone on smoothly sermonizing.)

After a moment's deliberation Joan decided to slip away for a while to the Coral Island, where the white-gold sand shone beside the warm tropical sea, where the breadfruit trees hung with large tins and cottage loaves, where the forests rustled with edible piglets and conversational parrots.

Once Joan had shared the island with its original inhabitants, sharp young Peterkin, who had joked his way into her heart; gormless Ralph, always doing things wrong; and that tiresome broad-shouldered know-all Jack, always correcting Ralph and rebuking Peterkin, and generally making rather a grown-up nuisance of himself.

The onset of puberty, however, had made this trio something of a liability. It was hard enough to cope with the maintenance of female secrecy back in London, so how could anyone manage the feat on a coral island? The only solution Joan had been able to come up with would be to make off alone into the forest every month, and find a stream to sit in for however many days and nights it took, and let the water carry away all the gory evidence.

But then eating and drinking would be next to impossible, and Jack, Ralph, and Peterkin might well wonder what on earth you were up to, disappearing like that, and feel duty bound to question you, or secretly follow you when you refused to answer.

No; it was no use; the only real way out of the problem had been to ship Jack, Ralph and Peterkin home where they belonged, and keep the island to herself. So Joan had reasoned, during many nights of insomnia, during her thirteenth year.

Alone now, as for many years, Joan added fresh water to Ralph's aquarium, and watched the crabs stealthily undress, and waded in the warm still waters of the lagoon.

Today she decided to watch out for the penguins, and of course they shortly arrived, hopping stiffly over the glittering pink coral rocks, playing leapfrog over the waves, and ring-a-ring-a-roses, flipper-to-flipper, in the creamy surf.

And why not? smiled Joan, making the penguins fly round in small circles about the palm trees, why not? Even when she was a child the mysterious presence of penguins on a tropical island had rather worried Joan. A whole troop of lotus-eating penguins idling away in the tropics, far from their proper icy homes! It was very odd, very odd indeed, so odd that Joan felt at liberty to make the penguins entirely fantastic creatures, capable of formation ballroom dancing, aerial displays, and, beaks skyward and quivering wings well back, choral singing of the utmost precision and charm, though their voices were a little on the squeaky side.

This afternoon the penguins played Follow My Leader, hopping stiffly all in step over the golden sand, up one side of a palm tree and down the other, skipping over the gleaming rocks and gracefully leaping Ralph's aquarium, and floating away one by one into the blue striped endless sea.

'Oh no!' cried Joan softly to herself, fingers covering her mouth. Ralph's aquarium had brought her own to mind. 'Oh no!' and she was plunged back to Dunnett Street, where luckily Cissie had been too angry about Social Security frauds to hear her. Joan's own aquarium: a waiting-room now, furnished the night before Lily's fall and forgotten ever since.

Four of the white Scandinavian chairs stood on each side of the tank, with a low table in the middle for the old copies of *Punch* and *Woman's Own*, and, at one end, a tiny flower-pot bearing a stiff little plastic aspidistra. For over a week those fish had been patiently waiting, and all the time Cissie could have discovered them. Though she probably hadn't discovered them yet, Joan reasoned, because if she had the whole family would know about the fish by now. But she'd be sure to sneak into Joan's room sooner or later, on some pretext, and ordinary unfurnished goldfish must be there to meet her prying eyes.

Joan put her sandpaper down and rose, rather stiff from crouching, to her feet.

'Back in a minute,' she called to Cissie, over the snappish tones of the bishop, who now seemed quite as roused as Cissie, despite his cloth.

'They should bring back the birch, that's what I say,' said Cissie, scrubbing at the wainscoting beneath the window as if to demonstrate the degree of energy with which the birch should be employed.

'Violence will only beget violence,' retorted the bishop, evidently stung.

'I'm just – you know,' said Joan on the threshold.

'Why don't you go and live in Russia then, if that's what you want, you old bath-bun!' shouted Cissie as Joan softly closed the door behind her and ran upstairs.

The water was cold. She rushed the furniture out bit by bit, drying it on the bed coverlet, and finally stowed it all safely away in the shoebox in the cardigan drawer.

As she closed the drawer Joan was startled for a moment to hear voices directly overhead. She got to her feet and stared anxiously up at the ceiling where the voices were coming from, and presently remembered Gareth and Jeff, and smiled to herself with relief.

'Daftie,' she told herself, 'you're a daftie.' As she reached her bedroom door it struck her that the voices sounded as if they might be angry. She paused, listening, her eyes fixed on the ceiling. Yes, there it was again, a rumble of anger, and a strange, shuffling thump-noise, as if someone were agitatedly crawling about on hands and knees. Were Gareth and Jeff having a row? wondered Joan rapturously. And what were they doing in the empty rooms, which by corporate decision (claimed Cissie) were to be left as they were, since they were hardly ever used.

Of course they might just be arguing with Cissie's bishop, thought Joan regretfully, closing her bedroom door behind her. Then she remembered that it was a long time since she had looked out at the view from the top-storey windows, and realized that it might be very interesting to see how London had changed through these familiar old frames. And so, ears wide open, she started quickly up the last flight of stairs, treading very softly so as not to miss anything.

FIFTEEN

'SEE, she was cunning,' recounted Joan in the special sing-song voice all her family employed to retell its legends, 'she spilt a whole pot of tea down the stairwell, said it was Cissie, and her too little then to deny it. But I saw her do it, see, I saw Mum do it. I used to watch her. And I saw her do it.

'Then she gets two men in to do up the stairwell again because of the stain. It was them papered over the cupboard; she must've told them to. Anyway I see her before the men came, taking off the cupboard door handle with a screwdriver.'

'Bit of a risk,' said Jeff, grimacing doubtfully, 'suppose they'd had a look inside?'

Joan jumped easily to her feet and began to stride up and down the little room, vibrant with excitement. She shook her head.

'She'd wedged it shut. She wedged it shut, I remember now!' Joan stood in the middle of the room, miming Lily's moves:

'A something folded, cardboard probably. She shut it in the cupboard door, hammered it to with a hammer. That's what I heard first. Before she unscrewed the handle. The men would've had to work to get that door open. And she'd have stood over them: Oh it's been jammed for years, the damp, no don't bother, just paper over the thing, will you, see?' Joan patted her hair, as Lily might have done, flirting companionably on the stairs in 1926.

'And they might've painted over the cracks, the decorating men. To get a smoother surface.'

'Didn't see any cardboard,' said Gareth morosely from the window, where he stood with his hands in his pockets and his nose against the glass. Five more minutes, he thought fretfully, five more minutes and I'm off. They can say what they like. Oh God. Good afternoon, Officer, I'm afraid I must report a crime. Good afternoon, Officer, I think a murder may have been committed. You're hardly going to believe this, Officer, but –

'Of course,' said Jeff, touching the closed lid of the box with one finger, 'we've got no proof that it was, you know, hers.'

Joan shook her head and sucked noisily at her teeth, considering. 'I just can't remember. Whether she looked different. But when Cissie and Jessie were born, I can't remember her looking different then either. Not like nowadays,' Joan added with a shade of distaste. Not like nowadays, she thought, when women went around looking more enormous than had been decent in the old days.

'Probably small-for-dates,' said Gareth distantly from the window. Five more minutes, he told himself again. But he did not check his wristwatch.

'What?'

'Small-for-dates.' Gareth turned round. Of course his uncle and aunt were not familiar with such a precise professional term. He cheered up a little. 'Small-for-dates. Of course you can't be sure, not when it's – mummified. But it looks a bit small: not fully grown. Small.'

'Premature?' fumbled Jeff. He stood up. Talking of the problem as a baby was painful, brought the infant Marion to mind. Had the thing in the enamel box once looked as

132

she had? Jeff's knees ached with trembling. His earlier detachment was eroding now that Gareth was calm and Joan so comfortably putting two and two together, to make whatever she pleased.

'Premature, you mean?'

'Not exactly.' There was hardly time, Gareth thought, to explain the difference now. 'Not exactly, but well, small.'

'Maybe that's why it died,' said Jeff hopefully.

'Could be.'

Joan sniffed. 'She fell downstairs. Often,' she said, looking at Jeff emphatically. 'Often.'

'If it died naturally,' said Gareth patiently, 'why did she hide it? There's no point in discussing it. Somebody hid a body. Therefore somebody killed someone. Right? We may as well all agree. Before we go to the police.'

Joan looked blank. 'The police?'

'I told him already,' put in Jeff. 'I said to him –'

'What we want to tell them for?'

'This is a police matter,' said Gareth stiffly.

'No it's not,' said Joan with conviction.

'Yes it is.'

'No it's not.'

'Yes it is. It *is*. Murder is. I'm going to the police and I'm going now.'

Gareth made heavily for the door. Joan waited until his hand was on the doorknob before she spoke, chattily, to Jeff:

'Look good in the papers, won't it?'

Gareth turned around.

'Oh they'll have a field-day; we'll all get our pictures in the papers.' She turned on Gareth and added fiercely, 'Just you think about that!'

Gareth took his hand off the doorknob and thought. The local rag first, of course. Probably headlines: Tragic Find In Hackney Stairwell. We will of course be making some kind of investigation into the circumstances of this very sad case, said a police spokesman last night. Dr Gareth Williams, 26, who with his uncle Jeff Corbett, 57, taxi driver of 11, Gawber Street, discovered the body whilst redecorating, declined to give any comment.

And a column or two, at least, in the national press. Human interest in the *Sun*, with a picture of the house-front, perhaps. Social comment in the *Guardian*. Perhaps even a quick shot of the whole terrace ('In this condemned and decaying back street') on BBC *Newsnight*, if other pickings were few.

And the nurses standing about in twos and threes: It was his grandmother did it, did the kid in, and all the family lived there ever since, imagine! Yes, Gareth Williams. She was on Unity ward, right old so-and-so apparently. Bit an aux. Just fancy . . .

Sudden silences when he appeared, thought Gareth. Oh, hah, hallo, Gareth! What are you up to these days, oh ah, I mean . . .

And Elizabeth, Elizabeth! I didn't think of Elizabeth, wailed Gareth internally. Elizabeth would be interested. After the first shock, Elizabeth would be enthralled. She would never stop analysing the evidence. He could almost hear her now, the angry half-shout she used in political arguments: 'What else can you expect from a desperate woman, that's what these Pro-Life wankers don't realize, a desperate woman will take desperate measures, children to feed, no money, no contraception, I ask you, what else could she have done?'

'Yes,' said Joan, as if she were commenting on his thoughts, 'Yes, you wouldn't like that, would you?'

Joan folded her arms, waiting. The prospect of publicity bothered her not at all. Why shouldn't people know what Lily was really like? Ah, Lily was a murderess, an infanticide. Lily was shrinking by the minute, Lily was shrivelling up into a little damned old soul, whose crimes were known, whose nasty secrets had fallen into younger, stronger hands.

Guard the secrets, or throw them to the winds; it was all one to Joan.

'Wool, are you off?'

Gareth sighed, and made up his mind. 'No, I er, hadn't thought of the publicity. I can see it would be very hard on, ah, on . . .'

'On her. On your grandma,' said Joan, nodding. Gareth looked at her sharply, but her face seemed empty of all sarcastic intent. 'And her so ill after all,' Joan finished. 'Poor old thing.'

Jeff and Gareth briefly met one another's eyes.

'Actually,' said Jeff, 'I don't want Cissie finding out about this.'

Joan's eyes gleamed with extreme pleasure, but she managed to say aloud, 'Oh, why not?'

Jeff shrugged. 'Don't want her worried. Anyway the fewer know about this the better. And I don't want her worried. She's too nervy as it is.'

'Nervy? Cissie?' Joan snickered with surprise and disbelief.

'She has a lot of trouble with her nerves. She has to take pills from the doctor.'

'*Cissie* does?'

'Yes, Cissie does,' said Jeff irritably. Of course this was what Cissie had always complained of in Joan, this inability to see what was going on right under her own nose. Lives in a world of her own, that was what Cissie always said. And, having managed to connect the old familiar Joan with the new and alarming manifestation before him, he was emboldened to take charge again, and added,

'Best keep your mum out of this too,' to Gareth, who sullenly shrugged assent.

'Right then,' said Jeff, looking round. 'We're agreed. We sort it all out ourselves. We, we get rid of it, right?'

'Better be fast,' said Joan with amusement, 'because

Cissie'll be up these stairs any minute.' She held up a finger and all three, listening hard, caught the faint sound of neutral music from the radio two storeys below. 'Any minute now.'

'Hide it,' said Gareth promptly.

Jeff looked round the bare room, desperately. Up the chimney? Out of the window?

'In my room,' said Joan. 'Nowhere else it can go.'

'But – we might have to leave it there – all night.'

'I know, I know. You think of something better, you tell me.' Arms folded, Joan leant backwards a little from the waist, Sister Burwash staring down a clumsy probationer.

Jeff hesitated.

'But Cissie wanted to stop here all night. To make an early start. You might have to have it in your room with you. All night.' Was it real, her calmness, he thought wretchedly, or would she snap later, run screaming up and down the street come midnight? Could you trust her or not? Nothing short of a million pounds would make him spend such a night himself.

'Jeff? Where is everyone? What you all up to?' From somewhere below them, Cissie's voice spiralled echoing up the stripped staircase. Resonance made its tone indecipherable. Teasing? Suspicious? Annoyed?

'Just coming,' yelled Jeff from the doorway, 'just a minute!'

'What choo up to?' The voice sounded a little closer.

With frenzied haste Gareth and Joan began to fling the parcel back together again.

'Gimme that curtain!'

'Oh Christ!' Gareth ran to the door. 'She's coming up the stairs!'

'Coming right now,' shouted Jeff, as Joan pushed past him. He wandered back into the middle of the room, and found that he was alone. 'Just coming.' Footsteps clattered briefly on the stairs outside. He held his breath, listening.

Cissie's voice. Must've met them on the stairs, but going in with it, or coming out without it?

'Time for a little breather,' he heard Cissie say. Normal voice; coming out without it, then. Thank God. Time to decide what to do next. He drew his sleeve across his forehead, and blotted his upper lip, thinking with passion of a cup of tea.

Something gritted under his feet as he moved. He looked down and saw a sprinkling of rust like little brown stars scattered at his feet. The sight made his eyes ache. A baby had, perhaps, looked its first stately look upon the world and the world had wrapped it in rubbish, and stowed it away in a cupboard like a piece of leftover cheese.

And here he stood, all alone in a room where the slender ghost of his own young self might, some nights, ride a silent rocking-horse beneath the pale lamplit window.

'Jeff, for Pete's sake!'

'Coming,' shouted Jeff hoarsely, and, stepping very carefully over the rust, he made his way to the door.

SIXTEEN

CISSIE had at first been inclined to sulk over tea. She should, she felt, have been told about the stairwell cupboard immediately, as soon as it had been discovered, not let in on the news a good fifteen minutes afterwards along with Jessie, as if she and Jessie held equal family consequence.

As a result of this slight she had determined not to be at all excited about Gareth's puzzling find.

'Isn't that strange,' she had remarked with a little nod and a gracious smile, when Joan had led her reverently up the last turn of the stairs. 'Very strange.' And she had turned with dignity and passed slowly down again, proudly indifferent.

It was odd though, that no one, excepting Jessie, seemed inclined to discuss the cupboard over their tea, and for a painful moment Cissie wondered whether they hadn't had a good long talk about it already, all three of them stood upstairs, while she, Cissie, worked all alone and forgotten on the living-room paintwork.

Then she had considered that, perhaps, there wasn't that much anyone could really say about an empty cupboard anyway, and been comforted. Still, just in case Joan had any notions about harping on the subject, Cissie resolutely told everyone about the jumper she was knitting for her elder son.

It was a complicated article and Cissie described her technique in great detail and at some length, since only Jessie made any attempt to divert her, and one lone voice was rarely enough to put Cissie off course once well under way.

Meanwhile Joan, sitting beside her sister at the table, felt as dangerously full of air as a pan of milk about to boil. A lifetime's suspicion vindicated, she thought joyously, hiding her smile in her teacup. That Lily was in reality a criminal, that she had broken the most solemn laws of her country, somehow proved that all the private domestic villainies, her overbearing selfishness, her evil tempers, all her unpleasant foibles from knocking the infant Jessie unconscious with a bottle-opener to a recent refusal to eat mince cooked the way Joan liked it, all were objectively, unquestionably true.

I've spent a lifetime half-believing I'd imagined her, Joan thought, full of strong gleeful happiness, as light and airy as a good meringue, and all the time I was right! How she used to sob and cry after she'd hit one of us, how she'd beg forgiveness and blame a drop too much or a bob too little; convincing us, convincing me, that the love was real, the blows an aberration. When all the time it was the other way about, O, evil Lily!

And Cissie knew nothing whatever about it. There she sat, poor fat old Cissie, nattering on about her knitting all unaware of the tremendous secret presently stowed beneath Joan's bed. Ah, it was too much, Cissie's ignorance, thought Joan; it was like a rich exotic dessert after an already intemperate banquet.

'Any more tea?' Joan asked Jessie suddenly in a loud whisper, hoping to defuse her own explosive thoughts. But as she spoke she seemed to feel her eyes bulge outwards in a strange way, all by themselves, as if her face, prompted by the strong pressures within, were breaking free of her mind's control. The feeling vanished so quickly that Joan at once doubted whether the strange bulge had happened at all. Had Jessie noticed anything? Hard to guess; after a quick peck of a look inside the teapot and an apologetic shake of the head, Jessie had turned back to Cissie, whose difficulties she actually appeared to be following.

'And the back on circular needles, you know the soft wire backs on the shorts, number threes.'

Joan laid her rattling cup and saucer down on the table and saw that she must leave the room, and quickly. She felt light, deliriously light and empty now, so light that at any moment she might soar bodily up to the ceiling and loop-the-loop in tight graceful curves.

'Excuse me,' she snorted abruptly. She stood up, and brushed away the biscuit crumbs from her skirt. The action felt awkward, comically brutish, as if she had momentarily exchanged arms with an orang-outang.

'Goodbye,' she called brightly from the door. The handle fumbled itself jokily in and out of her fingers for some time, at the end of which indefinite period the door, apparently acting on its own initiative, swung itself violently open, so that she almost fell through it, still smiling backwards into the kitchen.

'Whoops!' Then she was standing in the passage at last, the door slammed fast behind her, panting, still not laughing, not yet.

'Now then, now then,' she said sternly to herself, but with a bound her legs shot her along the passage and scampered her up the stairs, floor by floor, in hopeless flight from her own deplorable and, at last, quite uncontrollable laughter.

After a short silence, Gareth, understanding what an opportunity lay before him, sat forward, swung his left ankle onto his right knee, grasped the expanse of sock thus laid bare and, in his most subdued and professional tones, asked, 'How long has she been acting like this?'

So serious, so medical he sounded, that all his hearers quailed, and instantly became not-quite-sure what he had said. After Cissie, Jeff and herself had all looked searchingly at one another, Jessie spoke out.

'What – you mean funny?' Jessie was frightened. She had always liked to think of Joan as a harmless eccentric. Eccentricity was respectable, even a little classy. 'My sister's a dear,' Jessie would remind her neighbours before Joan's occasional visits to Kent, 'but she is a little eccentric.' And now here was Gareth implying that Joan was really mental, a nutcase, a lunatic. If he were right, as of course he must be since he was a doctor, then she, Jessie, was a woman who had a sister who –

Jessie swallowed.

'She's always lived in a world of her own,' declared Cissie stoutly.

'She's been a bit worse lately,' said Jeff, catching Gareth's eye. 'Don't you think she has?'

Cissie leant forward, forgetting her indignation for a moment. 'Hey, tell you what.' She giggled. 'She does some funny things with those goldfish of hers.'

'Yes?' said Gareth, clinically interested.

'Yeah. I peeked in her room, I forget what I was looking for, you know, something we needed. Anyway it was full of little chairs.'

'What was?'

'The goldfish tank. She's got goldfish. I looked in and I see all these little chairs. For the goldfish to sit in.' Cissie laughed indulgently.

'She always, you know,' said Jessie, getting braver, 'saw things as alive. All sorts of things.' She waved her small soft hands about descriptively. 'I saw her put a fairy – you know, a dandelion seed – out of the window once, last year this was. They're still fairies to her, see.'

'She's never grown up, not really,' agreed Cissie.

'No. Mum wouldn't let her.'

'Mum's fault as much as her own,' said Cissie piously.

'I agree,' said Gareth, still in character, 'that she's under a lot of strain right now.'

'The old lady so ill,' put in Jeff.

'But I wonder,' continued Gareth, 'whether she isn't really in need of help. Professional Help,' he added, looking meaningfully round the table.

There was a pause while this sank in.

'She seems to me to be definitely disturbed,' said Gareth smoothly.

'What, you mean a psychiatrist?' asked Jeff incredulously. Hold on, hold on, he thought. No need to go this far.

'She's upset, that's all,' said Cissie angrily. No sister of *hers* was being put away.

'You're taking it much too seriously, dear,' quavered Jessie.

'Psychiatrists,' said Jeff contemptuously, 'they're all mad themselves, ain't they?'

'Eccentric, that's all, she's just a little eccentric.'

Gareth wondered whether he hadn't, after all, overdone things slightly, and retracted. 'Well. I suppose you all know her better than I do . . .'

'That's just my point,' cried Cissie indignantly 'we *know* her better than you do!'

'But all the same, we ought to be, ah, gentle to her,' said Gareth carefully. Public suspicion must not be diverted. Joan must be its centre, Joan, whose oddities were already well-known: perfect camouflage for any later developments or corresponding peculiarities of Gareth's own, or of Jeff's. At any moment, Gareth reminded himself, any one of them might crack.

'Just keeping an eye out,' he added, with crafty vagueness. 'That's all I mean. That's all I'm going to do. For now.'

SEVENTEEN

'TOMORROW evening then.'

'About seven.'

'About seven, I says to Cissie. Here, me and Gareth are just popping out for a quick one.'

'You're sure Steve and Dave won't turn up?'

Jeff nodded. He was sure.

'And that's what you usually say? It's all got to be what you usually say.'

'What?'

'When you're off to the pub. Do you usually say to Cissie, "I'm just popping out for a quick one"?'

'Oh. Wool. I don't go out drinking. Not without her, anyway. We hardly ever go to pubs.'

'Oh great,' said Gareth bitterly. 'Won't suspect a thing, will she!'

'No, no. It'll be all right. Things have all been different lately.'

'The time all out of joint, you mean?'

'Er, yes, I suppose. You know what I mean.' Jeff looked sideways at his nephew. What was going on now? Not a minute ago he'd looked ready to cry, whereas now he was humming, scrubbing away at the stairwell paintwork with an actual grin on his face.

Trust me, thought Jeff glumly, to get into a mess like this with a couple like him and batty Joan.

'So anyway,' Gareth went on, 'off we go for a drink, and why not, after all this work.'

'Right.'

'In the car, because I'm taking you to my favourite colourful old cosy East-End-type pub, and it's too far to walk it.'

'And Joan's out?'

'Too right she is. Out.'

'She won't like it.'

'Don't suppose she will,' said Gareth, spitting on a knot in the wainscoting, and fiercely scouring it with his sandpaper. 'I don't-suppose-she-will. Oh, here, have you got a shovel?'

Jeff thought longingly of his garden shed, its warm smell of creosote, and the garden tools hanging head-down in neat rows. 'Got a couple,' he replied eventually.

'D'you do painting first, or papering?'

'Paintwork. Then it's easier. Doesn't matter about splashing the walls.'

'I see. And you agree about the quarry?'

Jeff sighed sadly. 'I still think it's too far. But I can't think of anywhere better.'

'Neither can I. I don't think we can risk anywhere in London at all. Too many cops. And this is a place I really know well.'

''Cept we'll be gone all bloody night. Talk about Cissie suspecting. Three-quarters of an hour just to get there, right?'

Gareth nodded.

'Half an hour digging. That's what, eight-fifteen, you're sure it'll be dark enough?'

'Of course it will.'

'Wool, eight-fifteen. Then another half-hour to make it look right afterward –'

'It's a sand-pit. A sand-pit. No one'll be able to see any difference. Could I start this bit now?'

'After a dust-down. All this dust, paint-dust, see? You'd get lumps in your surface. And no one goes down there?'

Gareth shrugged his shoulders. 'It hasn't been worked for years. Kids, sometimes. Kids play down there, I used to myself.'

'Kids? Oh my God. I don't want no kids finding that.'

'They're not going to find it. No one's going to find it. Now keep your hair on, or they'll hear you downstairs. We're going to bury it. It – it won't last like it has here. It –'

He noticed Jeff's expression and was silent.

'Got a brush?'

'Yes.' Jeff rubbed his face all over with his hands, his paintbrush under his arm. 'I can't hardly stand to think about it,' he cried suddenly. 'It makes me sick. The more I think about it the more I'm sure she done it in. I don't know,' he shook his head slowly. 'I was in the War, I was in Africa. But this. This is evil. It's evil, doing what she done.'

Gareth looked at his uncle with interest. There were, he thought, several layers of meaning in this outburst. There was the usual sentimental feeling for babies men of Jeff's age often seemed to share; there was also, perhaps, evidence of a more deep-rooted tendency, a male disgust for female misdemeanour; did not men like Jeff always judge women more harshly than they judged themselves? Was there, even, a strain of pure Victorian sexual disgust lurking somewhere in Jeff's small blinkered psyche? Not a doubt of it, thought Gareth cheerfully, working on the paint-tin with a tenpenny-piece. A function of class, after all. And age, of course.

'You don't know that she did anything,' he said reassuringly, laying a hand on Jeff's shoulder. 'Lots of babies died at birth in those days.'

'Had proper burials, too,' said Jeff, twitching free of the hand.

'Jesus, who chose this stuff?'

'Cissie did. And your mum. Let's have a look.'

'Ah well, I suppose I don't have to live with it.'

'It's not that bad.'

Gareth shrugged.

'Did you dust that bit down?'

'Yes, yes. I want to paint, I want to paint!'

'All right, all right ... Here. If someone, someone who knew. If someone who knew what to look for, did a, you know –'

'Post-mortem?'

Jeff nodded. 'Did a post mortem. Would they find out what it died of?'

'Doubt it.' Gareth stood back, narrowing his eyes at the wainscoting. 'Doesn't that look a bit orange to you?'

'No. Wool, a bit. Here. Listen.'

'Mm?'

'When people.' Jeff lowered his voice. 'When people do what she done. What I say she done. How do they do it? Usually?'

'Well,' Gareth blew his cheeks out in puzzled embarrassment. 'Well, come on, it doesn't exactly happen every day. Doesn't happen as often as it used to, I'm sure,' he added with a quick glance along at his uncle.

Indicating, thought Jeff indignantly, that his, Gareth's, generation is a big improvement over my lot. There were a host of good answers to the charge, Jeff thought: people had more money now; everyone had more money, even poor people. And all sorts of things were easier. No winking in barber's shops for the likes of Gareth. People knew more. Kids today were in control. And they could go to the doctor, and the doctor wouldn't say, Sorry dear, that's what Heaven must intend, he'd say, All right, we can fix that, come back next week, O.K. What people did nowadays, thought Jeff, was take advantage of the fact that an extremely small human being is easier to dispose of than a very small one. Instead of desperately burying their infant victims with their own hands, in secret graves or deep millponds, instead of madly walling them up in hidden cupboards, young folk nowadays could simply use mains sewage. A pull of the wrist, and all that unpleasantness flushed away for good.

Not lesser crime: easier disposal.

'You –' began Jeff at last, his speech all planned.

'I remember during Pathology,' interrupted Gareth, dabbing delicately at the skirting-board with his paint-brush, 'I took an old book out of the library, on criminal, ah, forensic pathology. Just out of interest. Very interesting it was too, though some of the pictures were a bit off. It had a whole chapter on infanticide, gave you the impression it was rife, simply rife. It was an old book, of course. Well before the Abortion Act. I should think that changed a few statistics, wouldn't you? That and the Welfare state, of course.'

'Wool –'

'But when people were really poor, really desperate, it must've happened all the time. Look at folklore, look at literature,' Gareth went on chattily, 'Somerset Maugham. Tolstoy. Look at the classics: Oedipus. Or Paris, even.'

'Paris?' repeated Jeff confusedly, as Gareth had rather expected he might.

'Or Romulus and Remus,' said Gareth, enjoying himself. 'The list's endless. When you think about it, infanticide's almost respectable.'

'Wool –'

'Usually smothered, according to this book. Or an over-dose of opiates, very easy to arrange. Though actually this book – the forensic pathology book – said that people often panicked, and overdid things. Real overkill, if you see what

I mean. It doesn't take much to kill a baby – you could just gently put your hand over its face – but in reality people'd panic and do all sorts of unnecessary and obvious damage. Strangle them, often with –'

'Oh, for Christ's sake be quiet!' hissed Jeff violently. 'You make me sick!'

'You did ask,' Gareth pointed out, offended.

Jeff let fly at the skirting-board with loaded paintbrush, leaving a fusillade of brownish dribbling blots on the plaster, as token of his anger.

'You, you didn't have to – you're enjoying it, you –'

'I'm simply trying to be detached. We must be detached about this. Or we may as well go to the police, no matter what sort of field-day the press has.'

'You just wait,' returned Jeff, nodding his head and still painting vehemently, 'you just wait until you've had kids yourself, and then let's see how you feel about it.' Which was not at all what he had wanted to say. He had felt some kind of radiance in his mind, a drawing-near of wisdom; and instead of battling to express it, he had somehow fallen back on a stock anger-response, one he had commonly employed for years against his own children, and so had himself quite forgotten what he had nearly enabled Gareth to understand. His anger faded and he sighed.

Gareth meanwhile had made a small but audible sound to indicate boredom and exasperation. It was the answer old people always resorted to eventually: Just You Wait. It was true enough, of course. Experience could only change you. But where was the use in pointing out the fact? Might as well describe autumn to the blind.

'Come on,' said Gareth at last, friendly with only a slightly evident effort, 'let's finish up this bit. And keep calm, right? Everyone should just keep calm.'

EIGHTEEN

IT was three in the morning, and Joan, fully dressed, sat upon her bed and thought. She had not liked to undress in the presence of the box. To do so would not only be lacking in reverence for the dead, but also faintly dangerous to herself, as if clothes were everyday armour. In films the victims of Dracula or other vengeful spirits were always wearing flimsy night-attire when their fates caught up with them – it was a sort of rule; so Joan felt almost invulnerable in her Marks & Spencer's heavyweight knit.

Not that she expected anything supernatural to emanate from the green enamel box, now stowed beneath the goldfish table. She had already tried communication, laid herself down on the bed, eyes closed, and mentally invited connection; but the thing in the box had made no response. Perhaps it had been too young to haunt. After all, Joan thought, why should it resent being dead, when it had clearly been too young to know it was alive?

Still, to be on the safe side, she had kept her shoes on too, the faster to run with should the thing in the box change its mind; she was compelled, also, to direct her thoughts at the box's contents, just in case something knowing lay listening there.

Was it because you were a girl? Joan thought. I remember her saying she was sick to death of girls, after three in a row. She wanted a son. Were you a fourth daughter? Was that why?

She could have swung for you, you know. She could have hung. That must've kept her awake a few nights.

Free of you now, though. I wonder when she stopped thinking about you. After ten years, after twenty?

Would they try her for murder now, when she and her crime were both so very old?

Surely not. Her little white head would just reach the top of the dock. Surely not.

But if they wouldn't arrest her, did that mean that crime itself could evaporate, after a certain number of decades had passed by?

If she'd had the sense to put you somewhere damp you'd be long gone. Long gone.

No body. No evidence. No crime.

It's very mysterious, Joan silently told the thing in the box. No crime. Because no one knew you. You had no personality, no name, no history, no friends, no acquaintances, no neighbours, no milkman, no local, no newsagent. No one. Like that riddle about a tree falling in the desert: would it make a noise falling, with no one about to hear the sound?

You had no one. You weren't ever really alive, as far as that goes. So how could you have been murdered? Like the tree in the desert: could a murder be said to have occurred, with no one, no one on earth, to miss the victim, or be affected by his loss?

But then Lily would have known. And that would be enough to make it murder. She knew you all right. She knew.

Doesn't now though. I'm sure of it. She stopped wondering about you long ago.

Except in her dreams. I've watched her struggling in her sleep. You've got her there.

Joan swung her legs round onto the bed, and lay down. She felt that she had said enough. She closed her hot eyes. Life was going to be very different. She smiled. It was a dream come true: Joan herself was going to be very different, a different, stronger woman, willy-nilly; with no efforts to make or peter out after a few weeks, leaving her limply the same as ever. Different. Stronger.

When shop assistants terrorized, or buses failed to stop, or post office queues remained stationary, Joan would never quail again, but remembering her own part in her mother's dreadful crime, would feel a great strengthening surge of vigorous excitement.

Daringly Joan kicked off her shoes, and pulled her dressing-gown over her feet to keep them warm. Was it possible to sleep, with the thing in the box not four feet away? Joan yawned, and thought that probably it was. Tonight she was strong enough for anything.

Downstairs beside Cissie on the sofa-bed, Jeff was dreaming. He stood in his dew-wet slippers on his own back lawn, his legs as heavy as a deep-sea diver's, watching the dead child turn over in its coffin, disturbed after its long sleep. He heard the rustle of its shroud, and opened his mouth to scream aloud, but before he could draw breath Cissie knocked her fist angrily on the kitchen window behind him, and bawled at him: What the hell did he think he was doing still stood about in the garden after all this time?

The nightmare resolved into a familiar domestic wrangle, and passed without even waking Jeff up.

Gareth, alone in his single bed a few streets away, dreamt that Elizabeth had told him she was pregnant. She sat beside him in their usual corner of the local, sorting through a hank of her long brown hair, looking for split ends.

'But you needn't worry,' she added in her light ironic voice, 'after all, it's only an anxiety dream.'

Sweating, Gareth awoke, discovered that his bladder was full, forgot what he had been dreaming about, and remembered what the past day had held.

Wide-awake, he shuffled to the bathroom and sat limply down on the toilet. Of all the places in the modern world which promote depression – laundromats, multi-storey car-parks, large low-ceilinged shopping centres with piped music, airport cafés – none can compete for depressive effect with a communal bathroom at four in the morning.

Gareth, leaning his head against the empty toilet roll, noted the multiple beige rings about the bath, and its horrid residuum of other people's stray pubic hairs; the cracked linoleum curled back to catch at the door; the ingeniously misaligned bolt, which by dint of much sweating and grappling could just be drawn, though at some risk of never being undrawn again; the flattened oval of bathroom mat, once a fluffy lime-green, never quite dry now, slimy with damp talcum powder and sharp with alien toenail clippings snared amongst the pile; and the sink, grey with grime, its walls apparently stubbled with a dark incipient beard, since someone – me, Gareth remembered bitterly – had emptied the collected shavings of a week or two down the side, and neglected to rinse the little specks away.

Gareth stood up when he had finished and splashed a little cold water over the sink's growth of stubble, which remained obstinately where it was. Finally he wiped some of it off with his fingers, drying his hand on someone else's towel, which consequently wore a little scattered beard of its own that morning, to its owner's later surprise and disgruntlement.

A long day coming, thought Gareth wearily as he stumped back to his sleepless bed. I'd make a cup of tea, if I could face the kitchen.

He sat down on the rumpled bed.

Can I face the bloody kitchen?

Gareth looked hard at the wall opposite.

Might as well.

Sighing, his dressing-gown hunched about his shoulders, Gareth creaked his way downstairs to put the kettle on.

NINETEEN

'HEADACHE?' Cissie looked disappointed, even hurt.

She's pictured us all three clustered about Mum's bed, thought Joan, her hand to her brow, and now I've spoilt her little day-dream. Poor old Cis. Doesn't she know yet that things never turn out as imagination plans them?

Not only the ambitious, castle-in-the-air-type fantasies either, but the small domestic type too, dreams of catching a certain bus tomorrow, or visiting a Whites sale, even these things never happen quite as they ought, thought Joan cheerfully.

'Oh dear,' added Jessie at the hall-stand mirror, where she was admiring her own brown new fur hat.

'I really need to lie down, I've felt a bit funny all day,' said Joan.

Cissie shrugged. 'Wool. I suppose we'll just have to go without you, then.'

Joan nearly smiled. Another time and I'd have been convinced, she thought. Another time, and she'd have made her disappointment mine. Not now, though, not now.

'It was you said we should go in the first place,' Cissie went on accusingly.

Aha, thought Joan. Trying another tack. Aloud she said,

'Wool, I still think we should. I mean, I wish I could. It's two nights now since we visited. I just wish I felt up to it, that's all.'

'Wait a minute.' Cissie stamped up the stairs past Joan and disappeared.

'She's a bit fed up,' mouthed Jessie as Cissie's cross footsteps faded. 'I don't know.' She turned back to the mirror and touched her curls with her ring-fingers. 'Everyone's been so out of sorts today. I don't think Jeff's at all well. You know. And Gareth nearly bit my head off this morning, I don't know –' she smoothed her eyebrows – 'I really don't.'

Cissie reappeared, standing square on the landing, huffy in her black-and-white dogstooth.

'I had a quick word with Jeff,' she announced ominously. 'He said he'd bring you up a cuppa later on.' She came smartly down the stairs, tugging on her tight black nylon gloves. She was still angry, Joan saw. 'You off to bed then?' Cissie demanded.

'Yes. I think so. Give her my love, tell her I'm sorry, won't you?'

'We won't be long,' said Jessie smiling lavishly from the doorway. 'Ooh, she doesn't look well,' Jessie went on as she unlocked the car door for Cissie.

Cissie shrugged and climbed stiffly inside. Everything, she felt obscurely, had gone wrong today. Nothing she could put her finger on, until this evening, with Joan crying off, but still, but still.

'You know what Jeff said to me?' asked Cissie aggressively as Jessie started up the engine.

'What then?'

'Him and your Gareth. He said. Might be popping out for a drink later on. The two of them.'

Joan, Cissie, Jessie and their brother Jim have never enjoyed a drink in their lives, having seen what the stuff could do to Lily.

'What they want to do that for?' Jessie felt mystified and

alarmed, as if Jeff and Gareth had proposed to go out after
dark and break windows.

'That's what I said,' replied Cissie, 'that's what I said. I
don't know. I really don't.' She realized anew that no one
ever told her anything important. 'Don't ask *me*,' she added
bitterly.

Jessie sighed. 'Shall I stop off at the corner shop, get her
some more of those blackcurrant bon-bons?'

Cissie sighed too.

'Yeah. Why not.'

With a suspense film or two in mind, Joan stood with her
ear to the door for a few minutes, until the sound of Jessie's
car-engine had blended with all the others on the distant
main road.

Then she turned and took the stairs two at a time to the
third storey. Jeff was sitting on the stairs, waiting.

'All set?' Joan asked, as she drew level.

Jeff got to his feet and tucked his left hand in his right
armpit, his right hand in his left armpit, and squeezed
miserably.

'Where's Gareth?'

Jeff jerked his head, indicating a lower floor. 'Down
there.'

The toilet flushed as he spoke, as if backing him up.
Gareth appeared on the landing.

'The coast's clear,' Joan called down to him. 'I think we
should start straightaway, don't you?'

Gareth stood very still by the bathroom door, one hand
on the doorknob, and looked up at his uncle. Jeff turned
away.

'Well?' asked Joan encouragingly. 'Ought to be off,
oughtn't we?'

Gareth let go of the doorknob, and nodded his head.
'Right,' he said.

TWENTY

JOAN sat in the back of the car, as seemed only natural for the female in the party, and hummed a jaunty little tune to herself, tapping one foot to the beat and supplying drumming-type sound effects between phrases.

No one spoke. Earlier, nosing cautiously out onto the Mile End Road, Gareth had wondered aloud about the neighbours.

'Are they going to think about the shovels – you know, remember us loading the boot?'

Joan had been a little puzzled. 'We ain't got any neighbours,' she had answered, 'they're all black.'

And that had been that, as far as conversation went. Joan looked out of the window as she hummed, and saw a row of nice private houses, all with little dark gardens, and windows daringly left uncurtained, as if the owners were saying proudly, Go on then, look in, admire!

Be lovely at Christmas, Joan thought, to drive down this road and see all the little trees with their lights on. She peered searchingly into each passing creamily lit front room. A pine bookcase, looks shoddy. A TV flickering, wonder what's on, is it the film by now or still the hymns?

'Where are we?' Joan demanded abruptly, leaning forward.

Gareth jumped. He had been jumping all day.

'Sidcup.'

'Oh.'

Funny-looking lamps, pink bendy ones, wouldn't have them. A cat on the windowsill, curled and sleeping. Maybe I'll get a cat now. I'd like a cat. A man with a beard, holding a book. Unusual. You don't often see the people, they stay out of sight, it's their decor they want you to see, not themselves. Just their little stage, not the play itself.

The row of houses ended, and the lamp-posts seemed to grow brighter. Often now Joan could make out her own face in the dark mirror of the car window, its shape sharply focused, the eyes glinting liquid shadows.

Enjoying yourself? the eyes seemed to ask, ironically. I've spent my whole life looking at things, thought Joan, seeing this dark mirrored face. It was what I was told to do: Look at that man, Joanie, ain't he got a funny nose! Look at that little house, nice isn't it, see my new coat, Joanie, look at this, look at that –

They just show you things, thought Joan, and they expect you to make something out of it. I spent my whole life just looking. You can look but you can't touch. A long trip to a museum, that's what it's been, thought Joan, a long trek round the glass cases, just looking.

Can I help you, madam?

No thanks, I'm just looking.

Just looking, jeered Joan's own image, flashing intimately into Joan's eyes as the lamp-posts waxed and waned like rows of little moons. Just looking.

Joan slowed her jaunty song down to dirge-tempo, and was immediately diverted; sung slowly the tune became recognizable, developed words. Lily had sung it to her long ago, a tender Lily singing her child to sleep with a sad gentle lullaby:

> My old man said follow the van,
> And don't dilly-dally on the way . . .

'Going up the A20?' asked Jeff suddenly, breaking his long silence. He kept his hands snugly beneath his armpits still, and every now and again gave them a brief hard squeeze.

'Yes,' said Gareth, jumping.

'What, past Brands?'

'That's it.'

'You ever go there?'

'Brands Hatch? No.'

There was a pause.

'Funny that,' Jeff went on. 'You living so close and all.'

'Not really interested in speed,' said Gareth loftily. Suppose we get stopped, he thought, quaking. Suppose I jump a light or wobble the steering. Just suppose.

May I see your licence, sir?

Blow in this here sir, will you please, sir?

Mind opening the boot, sir?

And what's all this here, sir?

'Sensible,' said Jeff, squeezing his hands tightly.

Dillied and dallied, lost my way and don't know where to roam, thought Joan, in time to her humming.

'This quarry,' said Gareth, clearing his throat. 'It's pretty safe. I didn't tell you, I forgot, it's going to be filled in. In about a year. They're going to be filling it in, packing it all down. Going to build houses on it.'

'Oh,' said Jeff. He thought of the baby buried miles down, weighted with tons of whatever it was they filled quarries in with, buried deep as a dinosaur in the layered earth. And of houses rising on top, with people living in them, hanging out the washing and walking the dog, and throwing parties, and not knowing, never imagining, what might lie so far beneath them in the new-packed ground.

You just stop that, Jeff thought sternly to himself. Stop that. Get a grip on yourself. He squeezed his hands yet more tightly. Stop that. All the earth's a bone-yard. London lies on plague-pits; who cares? No one cares, thought Jeff to himself. No one.

Jeff sighed. But I'll know about this one. And that will make all the difference. I've seen it, and I'll know it's there.

Wool you can't trust a copper like an old-time special when you can't find your way home, thought Joan sadly.

'Near your mum's, is it, this place?' asked Jeff.

'About two miles away. No one lives near. It's a bit cold for poachers, too.'

'Poachers?' Jeff smiled. In this day and age?

'Kids. Get rabbits. That sort of thing.'

Jeff was silent, marvelling at the ways of rural life. Out catching rabbits in the deepening twilight?

'Did you do it?'

'Me? God, no. Not my idea of fun at all.' For a nasty moment Gareth was nine years old again, watching his friend carefully shoot at a pigeon, a grey soft thing which had flown limpingly away into nowhere, the dreadful lump still lodged beneath one wing. He had cried as he told his mother about it, and Jessie had said that she'd never liked that Tony much anyway, which had made Gareth feel rather worse.

'Countryside,' said Joan brightly from the darkness behind him.

Gareth turned the car off the main road, and down a lane. The banks flowed evenly beside the car, greening in the lights and blackening behind them. Turning her head Joan saw black trees against grey sky, and a few frosty-looking stars. The lane twisted beside trees, crossed a stream. A cottage loomed and quickly foreshortened itself away. A white-faced dog stared from a hedgerow and barked once.

'Know your way about these places, eh?' said Jeff. The darkness and narrowness of the lanes disturbed him. They had not met another car for miles. He felt the empty countryside press in around him. Even in the warmth of the car he seemed to feel the chill of cold trees at night, and black wet grass.

I hate the countryside, thought Jeff, with sudden conviction. He remembered Sunday summertime rides out with Cissie, the trudging about wet gnat-ridden orchards for pick-your-own plums, and paying two quid a time to hang about some old ruin with the only decent habitable bits all corded off.

Cissie was all for retiring out to Essex, to be near Steve and Dave and, now, Marion. Well, she could go on her own, said Jeff to himself angrily. I was born a Londoner, he imagined himself thundering, and I'm bloody well going to die one! That'd shake her, if I talked like that. That'd shake her.

Shake me too. Returned to himself, Jeff smiled in the darkness. Shake me too.

The engine stopped. Gareth turned off the lights, and the sky instantly paled.

'We're here,' said Gareth.

TWENTY-ONE

'SEE her,' said Lily at last, opening her old tortoise eyes and inclining them towards the patient opposite, 'she's got fleas.'

Cissie stopped chewing her bon-bon. Jessie looked up from the backs of her hands, which she had been closely inspecting for several minutes past.

'Who, her?'

Lily nodded. 'Her with all her visitors,' she said sneeringly. The patient opposite was invisible behind the circle of backs bent solicitously about her.

Jessie thought she understood. She's upset because we didn't visit yesterday, she told herself remorsefully, and she looked across the bed at Cissie to see whether Cissie understood too.

But Cissie had half-risen in her attempts to see the patient opposite between the visiting throng.

Why don't you stand on your chair? thought Jessie at her, across the bed. Cissie felt nothing.

'How d'you know?' she asked her mother, sitting down again.

'Heard 'em talking,' said Lily, 'they all think you're deaf

or daft round here.' She paused, considering. 'Most of 'em are, too,' she added.

'Marion'll be in tomorrow,' said Jessie tenderly.

'Washing her down with some kind a poisonous soap, the dirty old bitch,' said Lily with relish. 'They ain't told her family yet. All that lot.' She grinned. 'Like to see their faces.'

Jessie stole a quick glance over her shoulders at the crowd about the opposite bed. They all looked quite respectable too.

'Remember Jimmy in the War,' she said suddenly, 'going from one depot to another, inspected both ends, and when he got on the train he was clear, and when he got off it at the other end he'd got fleas? Remember that?'

Of course they remembered. It was the tale of Jimmy and the Seat-Back.

'I never lean back on the train, I taught all the kids not to as well, all that nasty grease too,' said Cissie.

'Inspections at school, remember?' said Jessie, 'those O'Haras always had nits.'

'You could tell,' Cissie told her mother, 'because they used to have to have their heads washed in this special stuff, used to make their hair all stringy.'

'Remember Joanie scrubbing us.'

'Boiling hot water too –'

'Used to scream blue murder –'

'Green soap in your eyes.'

'Not like nowadays.'

No, not like nowadays, agreed Cissie. Nothing then was as it was nowadays. All the details of life were so much easier to get on with. Little things, like washing your hair, or cleaning saucepans, or laundering bed-linen. Feminine details; the sort of thing you never saw people do on the television.

Cissie sat silent, struggling with this confusion of original thought. 'It's –' she began, thinking she might unravel the tangle by putting it into words.

'They bringing the tea round yet?' asked Lily, craning her neck.

'Can't see it,' said Jessie.

Cissie subsided. Perhaps after all she had really had nothing to say. Best not to risk it anyway, she told herself, as she had often told herself long ago, as a schoolgirl. Though what exactly it was that she was putting at risk she hardly could have said, then or now.

'See that,' said Lily, glinting beneath her sly eyelids, 'giving her chocolate. She's on a diet, see?'

'What, the one with fleas?'

'No, no, her over there in the corner. Put them in her locker, see that?'

'She don't miss much,' said Cissie.

Lily was pleased. 'I don't miss a thing,' she said.

'They said anything about going home yet?' asked Jessie.

Lily made a little clicking noise in her throat, as if she were about to answer, and then was silent. Her eyes closed, the eyelids thick and smooth with age.

Jessie hesitated. She reached out a hand and touched Lily's limp round arm.

'Mum?'

'I'm tired,' murmured Lily.

Jessie made a quick perplexed-face at Cissie, who made one back in reply.

'She all right?'

'I don't know. Mum, Mum!'

Lily felt no pain. She was listening to the strange jungle rhythms of her own disordered heart. The blacks must be throwing another party, she thought dimly. Far away her children were calling,

Mum . . .

. . . Mum . . .

like a lot of bloody seagulls. Just having children, that was

164

all life had been. Though it had felt like something else at the time, hadn't it?

Lily opened her eyes, for the last time, and saw her daughters' white struck faces. Something very odd had happened. Between her fingers, that lay so neat and lax upon the coverlet, she had felt the cleanly rub of sand.

For a moment she tried to rouse and speak the word, questioningly. Sand?

Lily closed her eyes again, and, unsurprised, found herself in the sand-box in the park, a child again, digging with a small tin spade.

Her mother sat on a bench nearby, smiling under her big shady hat, and very faintly through the trees came the Sunday sound of a brass band.

Lily made careful palm-prints in the sand, and rested her weight upon her hands, her arms stiff little struts.

The sunshine was very bright, the light so clear that Lily could easily feel the smell of new hair-ribbons and the sound of her mother's good kid gloves.

Then there were wooden stairs to climb, safest on all fours, turn on the landing and smile down.

Wait for me, lovey, now then, where's that key?

TWENTY-TWO

GARETH, leading the way, held a small torch, which he shone at the muddy grass before his own feet, and behind him Jeff carried the enamel box. At first Jeff had held the box by the handle, like a suitcase, but once or twice it had swung hard against his legs, and the thought that it might burst itself open, despite its encircling strings, and fill his shoes and trouser turn-ups with its unspeakable flaking contents, had overcome his initial reluctance to hold the thing close to his chest. He carried it now, stiffly, under one arm.

Joan stumbled along behind him, a shovel in each hand, her eyes on the flickering torchlight ahead, on Gareth's feet in blue-and-white plimsolls, and Jeff's in brown lace-ups. Everything else was in various shades of chilly grey; dark grey hedgerows, paler grey sky. It was certainly a new experience, thought Joan, this marching in Indian file over a dark flat Kentish field at dead of night. She stifled a giggle.

'Wossat?' Jeff hissed, fierce with terror. A dark shape had breathed at him from beneath the black nearby trees. Something had snuffed the air, seeking for him. He stood rigid, right arm clamped helplessly about the box.

'It's a cow,' said Gareth bitterly into the night.

'What, they leave 'em out all night?' Joan was not convinced. 'All by themselves?'

Gareth turned and walked on, not bothering to reply.

'You'd think they'd run off,' said Joan conversationally. Jeff looked at Gareth's hunched shoulders in outline ahead. He wished he had not sounded so frightened about the cow. He thought back, listening to himself. He'd sounded frightened all right. 'Wossat?' He wished he had said something more now, something jocular, such as, 'Frightened me to death, that did!' or, 'Didn't half make me jump!' or something, anyway, to show how brief, how momentary, his fear had been. But it was too late now.

'Wouldn't you? Think they'd go off?'

'Ssh,' whispered Jeff, turning his head. 'Best be quiet, eh?'

Ahead Gareth's heartbeat was slowing quickly down to almost normal. The cows had scared him too, looming suddenly out of the dark like that. Somehow, he consoled himself, cows at night were disturbing creatures. Being out on their own at night seemed to give them a new identity, very different from the familiar image of rustic tranquillity they represented by day. No, thought Gareth, these cows were separate and inscrutable beasts, leading private independent night-time lives in which humanity had no part.

Interesting that Aunt Joan had pictured them wandering off rather than, say, being stolen. Evidently she too had felt the night-time cows belonged to no one but themselves.

Turning, Gareth flickered the torch quickly over the nearest specimen. It stood motionless, a smooth brown expanse of ribs, its pale face turned towards him, watching the strangers, interested and unafraid and clearly part of the freemasonry of the wild-animal world, from which mankind is excluded.

There was something terrible and pathetic, thought Gareth now that his fright had calmed, about the night-time autonomy of cattle. Their day-time passivity accorded better with their usual slaughterhouse fate. Except that –

Gareth thought of the cattle-trucks that rattled about day-time London, and the rows of broad noses set between the wooden bars, the eyes glimpsed pressed to the light. Their day-time passivity evidently lay in the eye of the beholder, thought Gareth, and saw himself drawn up at a red traffic light beside a cattle-truck, unable to ignore those noses and those large blind stares.

We need to think that they are passive and uncomprehending, thought Gareth, beginning consciously to rehearse his theories for Elizabeth; of course we prefer to believe them so. And by day, in fields, they look the part. But it's nonsense, modern nonsense for urban carnivores. An ambulance charging through the streets might spell out mortality; a skull turned in your fingers might speak to you of death; but for an image of fear, of fear-of-death, you can't touch a loaded cattle-truck, concluded Gareth.

He straightened his shoulders and strode forward more confidently over the battered autumn grass. All in all, he told himself pleasedly, taking everything into consideration, I really don't feel too bad at all.

'Look!' he cried excitedly at the trees to his left. 'See it?'

'What, what?'

Gareth pointed. 'Owl. Over there. See it?'

Jeff squinted into the moving darkness. Then all at once he saw the bird, sitting upright on a branch, it shape blunt and club-like. The club spread wings, lifted itself, and embarked upon the air, swinging round in a completely noiseless arc to disappear over the black line of tree-tops.

'Oh!' Joan was thrilled. 'I've never seen an owl before!'

'Absolutely silent,' said Gareth, pleased and proprietary. 'So they can swoop down on things,' he explained.

'Bit creepy,' said Jeff jocularly, 'if you didn't know what it was.' In truth the bird's soundless flight, its heavy silent wings, had made the skin over his spine bristle with horror.

'Much further to go?' he asked, wretchedly aware of the transparency of the question.

Gareth let the query hang in the air for a moment or two, so that no one could doubt his inner response to it. 'Nope,' he said at last.

They trudged on in the rustling countryside quiet. Gareth's mind presented him with a dismal little tune to march to. Presently he became aware of it. Now, what is that? Gareth asked himself, but the melody vanished almost completely as soon as he tried to listen properly, leaving only fragments of itself behind to vex him. Gareth scowled and tutted and hummed phrases over to himself. What was it? Something sad, something about being lost, oh, what the *hell* was it?

Behind him Jeff imagined the fat resilient squelch of slugs caught underfoot; he thought of snakes coiled listening round tree-trunks, of centipedes and blind heavy worms.

'Here we are,' said Gareth abruptly, halting. The sky seemed lighter behind him, the ground very flat beyond. He was standing at the edge of something, Jeff realized. 'The quarry. We go down here. It's not steep.'

But it was soft and crumbly. The solid earth had vanished, leaving sand, cold night sand as soft and dark as brown sugar. The air smelt different. A faint sound enlarged itself as they worked their way downhill, and became recognizably that of thin water passing over pebbles.

'Used to play here a lot when I was a kid,' Gareth volunteered as the soft ground levelled under their feet.

'It's not what I expected,' said Joan, puffing after him. 'I thought it would be empty.' She had imagined a moonscape: stark edges of sand sculptured by the wind like pictures of the Sahara. And here she was in a sunken garden. Young trees waved slenderly all about.

'I used to dam this, with sticks and rocks.' Gareth stepped across the little stream. 'Over there it cuts through sand.

Looks like the Grand Canyon in miniature. Waterfalls. Alluvial plains. The lot.'

As Jeff crossed the stream Gareth turned and gently took the box from him by the handle.

'My turn. You okay?'

'Fine,' said Jeff.

'Used to be quicksand over that way,' said Gareth, swinging the box to his right. 'Or so we used to pretend.' He remembered Bill Fortune climbing panic-stricken out of his wellingtons, leaving them stuck fast in the sticky sand. They'd gone back later that day and the boots had disappeared. 'Sucked in!' Gareth had told his mother, to frighten and impress her. 'Pinched,' Jessie had sniffed.

'I dug up a tree here, when I was eight,' said Gareth, 'dragged it home, Mum put it in the front garden. Now it's bigger than the house.' A childhood haunt, he was thinking. A childhood haunt; I never knew I had one until now. I never realized that I had had a childhood; I must have grown up at last.

'A pussy-willow tree,' he added, sighing. 'Lots of oak trees here too.'

'And they're going to fill all this in?' Joan asked.

'Yes. Fill it full of rubbish. Pack it all down. All those trees. And flowers too in summer. Dog daisies, vetches. Birds. Sand martins, make holes in the sides. And foxes, there's a fox-hole near the path we came in on.' All doomed, thought Gareth painfully. Part of my childhood gone: no visiting rights. The trees waved their strong young branches as if their days were still unnumbered. Gareth thought of the independent night-cattle in the pasture above, as calmly undisturbed as these young trees. As if this were simply another night, and not one night closer to the end.

'About here, I thought.'

The other two caught up.

'Here?'

'Yes. Sand's still sand—no grass cover I mean. So it won't

notice afterwards. The sand's got footprints all over it already. People take their dogs here for walks, you see.'

'Don't like the dogs,' said Jeff.

'Give me that spade, will you? Thanks. Look,' Gareth took up a shovelful of sand. 'We'll dig deep. And who could say how long it's been here, who put it here, even if it was found? Look, I've thought it all out, right?'

Something in the trees above them briefly screamed.

'All right,' said Jeff.

TWENTY-THREE

IN the waiting-room Cissie closed her eyes for a moment to concentrate on her own inner disturbance. Her mind seemed to be full of unfocused noise, a low-pitched surging hum as if somewhere close by a hall-full of anxious people were murmuring together.

This was what it was like when your mother died, thought Cissie.

Here and now the night my mother died.

Yes, it was about the time my mother died.

Did you know my old mother had died?

I'm missing that Robert Mitchum film.

Cissie popped her eyes open, and remembered that shock does strange things to people.

I must think, she told herself, but it was like trying to write letters at a party. The surges of inner noise pushed and jostled her, knocking her off course, bouncing her from one subject to another.

Marion'll be back soon, poor kid, and they must've gone out for that drink already, you'd think five minutes' solid ringing'd wake her up though, wouldn't you, hope she's all right, where do I claim her things from? Cissie created a tall bespectacled lady in a high-necked nylon blouse, and set her in a wooden kiosk somewhere near Reception.

Mrs Lily Lorrigan's things, please, I'm her next-of-kin, Cissie said to the bespectacled lady.

The form please, said the bespectacled lady. Lily's belongings, parcelled in brown paper, lay stacked on a table behind her.

What form, cried Cissie desperately, no one told me about the form!

And Marion ought to come to us for the first Christmas, that's only right, and I wish we'd been able to get hold of Jim when she first took ill –

'Oh!' groaned Cissie aloud, plagued by this tangle of thought, 'Oh!'

'Mm?' Jessie looked up.

'I can't keep still,' said Cissie over the hall-full of chatterers. She jumped up and began pacing the little room. The random noises seemed to fill her muscles and set them thrilling.

'My legs are screaming,' said Cissie, 'you know what I mean?'

Jessie was silent. She had been thinking of a song Gareth had learned as a Wolfcub, and sung to himself on long car journeys when he was a child.

> There were ten in the bed
> And the little one said
> Roll over! Roll over!
> So they all rolled over
> And one fell out,
>
> Nine in the bed
> And the little one said
> Roll over! Roll over!
> So they all rolled over
> And one fell out –

We've all rolled over, thought Jessie, and Lily's fallen out. Now it's me, my generation, on the very edge this time.

'My legs are screaming, you know what I mean?'

'What the hell are they playing at back there?' shouted Jessie, showing her teeth.

Cissie was startled. 'Eh?'

'Stuck in here waiting, what do they think they're doing to her!' Jessie folded her arms tightly and crossed her legs. The toes of her right foot, which alone still held contact with the floor, rocked her fiercely to and fro on her little orange chair.

Cissie knelt down beside the chair and laid one arm across Jessie's shoulders, which felt as unyielding as metal, as if poor Jessie wore a suit of armour-plating beneath her nice pink jumper.

Cissie kissed her sister's cheek and stroked Jessie's tidy perm with her fingers.

'There, there.'

'Oh, Cis!' Jessie unclenched her fists, and, tensely at first, allowed herself to cry. She turned her head and leant against Cissie and as she did so Cissie's inner hubbub died away.

'There, there,' Cissie, relaxed, comfortably stroked and patted.

Jessie's whole body unclenched itself and she cried with more abandon. She was aware, however, that she was cheating, that her grief was misinterpreted. Perhaps it was always so; who could ever unriddle another's grief correctly? And poor old Cissie always got things wrong.

At the thought of poor old Cissie always getting things wrong, Jessie lifted up her voice and cried like a child, and Cissie, luxurious in her silence, held her tightly in her arms, and rocked her gently, as if she were one.

TWENTY-FOUR

FOOTPRINTS left here in the soft sand had trickled their edges away, left the ground dimpled with rounded depressions, like the troughs of waves. The torchlight caught the little waves and deepened them. With her eyes half-closed Joan could imagine she saw the sea, frozen in tones of gold and black, stretching far beyond the strange scene at her feet, where two men, two shadows in the torchlight, hopped in and out of a grave, propelling fans of sand into the air like a pair of eager dogs.

The sand fell onto itself with soft slapping noises, like the soft dull sounds a woman's hand makes, patting a feather pillow into shape.

'How's it going?' Joan inquired, so as to feel involved.

Jeff was breathing heavily. 'Stuff's like bloody concrete down here.'

'What time is it?' Gareth asked, straightening up. He drew the back of his hand across his forehead, leaving it gritted with particles of sand. Joan turned the torch onto her wristwatch like a professional spy.

'Five minutes past nine,' she announced to the black dark.

'Jesus.'

'We'll have to leave it at this,' said Jeff, 'we can't stay here much longer, they'll be back.'

'Yes, yes,' said Gareth irritably. He was remembering something, a scene from his childhood, something that had itched in his memory all day.

'You've been in that quarry again!' Jessie had cried.

'No, Mum –'

'Don't you lie to me, look at your knees!'

Yes, that was it: this sand left stains. It was not seaside sand, that scrubbed away in the salt waves, or rasped pleasantly between clean dry toes after a day's castle-building. It was earthy sand, that stained skin and clothing with a deep bright yellow.

'Give me that torch a second, will you?' Gareth swung the light at his own front. Far above him a strolling fox saw the bright human figure leap into being from nothingness, and froze itself with awe and terror.

'Oh my God!' wailed Gareth, unaware of his distant thunderstruck audience. His jeans were splashed with deep yellow, the knees damply brown. He turned the torch on his uncle. Jeff blinked his gritty pale-yellow eyelids in the glare; his cheeks were lightly jaundiced, his shirt-collar ringed with gold. His trousers, like Gareth's, blazed with orange and brown stripes.

'Oh my,' breathed Joan, 'you do look a mess!' and she curled one hand snugly over her mouth the better to contain her shocked laughter, though an irrepressible snort or two still flattened itself against her fingers. Her shoulders shook.

Jeff drew a deep breath. 'We finish now. We get back, before them. We get cleaned up.'

'Suppose they're back already?'

'We go home – you go home, I go home. We wash up, change. You could stay home. I go back. I drove you home, Joan came along for the ride, see?'

'Won't work. I brought my car.'

'All right,' conceded Jeff, 'we took two cars when we went for the drink, dropped yours off at your house, went for the drink in mine, I took you home and Joan came along for the ride, see?'

'What did we go back to Grandma's house for?'

'You forgot something. I don't know, I don't know!' shouted Jeff suddenly. 'Let's just get on with it shall we, work it out later, all right?'

Gareth nodded. 'All right.'

Joan bent and picked up the enamel box. 'Here.'

Gareth took it, wedged it in the hole, leant on it with both arms and finally rammed it down to the bottom with a small jarring thud. He stood up sweating and picked up his shovel.

'O.K.?'

'No,' said Joan. She knew exactly what to say next, had been rehearsing it all through the digging. 'Shouldn't we – say a few words?'

Jeff immediately felt much better, more relaxed. Some unconscious part of his memory recognized Joan's words and, showing him pictures of reverent cowboys standing about open graves with their stetsons pressed over their hearts, told him that even unorthodox and unsanctified burial had its precedents, had its rituals, which, if survivors were to be comforted, must be followed in every detail.

Jeff shuffled his feet and bowed his head. 'Reckon you're right,' he said.

Gareth felt like groaning aloud. He had recognized Joan's words himself, with something like fear. Was any impulse, he asked himself, to be trusted, when the source of so many reactions and desires was clearly Hollywood, or Pinewood, or the BBC? He remembered his own mental reactions on first seeing the hidden cupboard. We're all film-buffs nowadays, thought Gareth, whether we know it or not: understanding others is a question of remembering the same screenplays.

Why, it was worse than medieval papism, this stranglehold secondhand imagery had on the modern mind. We think with minds wreathed about with celluloid, Gareth told himself. How can man ever have free will, Gareth wondered wildly, when he never knows whether or not he's quoting from *The Guns of Navarone*?

'This baby,' said Jeff, embarrassed but righteous, 'was probably done to death. It was a long time ago, it would have been getting on a bit now. It missed all its life. It wasn't our fault, we're just giving it a burial like it should've had years ago. God help it, and God help us too.'

'Amen,' said Joan. She crouched down beside the coffin and, opening up the little silk bag she had so handily come across that morning in the bottom of the wardrobe, sprinkled the dried lavender inside it over the enamel. It was ancient lavender, perhaps twenty years old. A faint scent arose from it as she rubbed it free of the little bag's corners, a very faint cool scent like the ghost of a summer evening. The flowers were so faded that they hardly wore any colour at all. They scattered on the coffin lid, as fragile as meringue.

It was fitting, Gareth saw, to scatter long-dead flowers upon this ancient child.

Fitting, original. The originality of it pierced him, made his eyes burn. And that's why we need the secondhand, he thought, as his nose began to run. He snuffled into his shirtsleeve. Familiarity dulls pain as well as pleasure, Gareth told himself, you can see why we need it.

Drawing conclusions dried his eyes. He swung his shovel into the heap of dug-out sand.

Jeff mopped his wet face with his yellowed handkerchief and found his own shovel.

The box was quickly covered.

Joan thought some last valedictory thoughts at the thing inside.

You were really my half-sister, like Cissie and Jessie. They don't know that. But you do. I was born before she was married, see, that's why she's never liked me, no matter how I tried. She probably always wished she'd done to me what she did to you. Perhaps she should have done. Perhaps it should've been me in there all the time.

'Back by ten?' Gareth puffed, busily sweeping sand across with the sides of his stained plimsolls.

'Should be.' Jeff stamped over the burial place, making authentic-looking prints to match the others dinted all about.

'Right then. Come on. Aunt Joan. Aunt Joan! Come on, we're all finished here. All right?'

Joan gave her shoulders a last shrug at the thing in the box. She turned round.

'Fine,' she said, and smiled.

TWENTY-FIVE

GARETH and Elizabeth, eating curry with forks, were sitting in Elizabeth's bedroom, watching Elizabeth's small black-and-white television.

'The whole thing's ridiculous,' protested Gareth from the floor where he sat at Elizabeth's feet. 'What does it think it's playing at? Why doesn't it go off and hide somewhere?'

'Don't ask me,' said Elizabeth absently, her eyes on the screen.

'All they've got to do is bomb it anyway. Call the RAF in. Why don't they call the RAF in?'

Elizabeth made no reply.

'It's always the same,' Gareth complained, 'with these alien invaders. They just can't concentrate: they always get side-tracked. You'd think they'd learn. Like football players watching replays; you'd think they'd learn from their mistakes. When trying to take over the world, you have to concentrate. You'd think they'd study the form, you'd think –'

'Oh do shut up,' urged Elizabeth, still watching.

Gareth, still watching, probed his curry suspiciously.

'Did you put marmalade in this?'

'Only a little bit. Do shush.'

Gareth sighed. 'I hate marmalade.'

'Sorry, I forgot.'

'Ha! Look, see! The RAF. What did I tell you! Why didn't they do that hours ago! I'd have done that hours ago.' Something stirred in Gareth's memory as he spoke. Warily, because his memory had lately developed a new habit of sneaking up on him unawares and dealing him momentarily blinding slaps when he least expected them, Gareth looked backwards and remembered the Woman Who Buried Half Her Father, and his own resultant conclusion that the stories people like to hear most are the stories which allow them to think, I'd have done differently, I'd have done better.

As I just did, courtesy of the BBC, thought Gareth. It was, perhaps, a function of most modern fiction, written or filmed. Gareth looked at the television, where the giant alien Krinoid frantically waved its tentacles. A mere formula, he thought: the film-characters were made to delay realizing the obvious course until all the viewers had time to realize what the obvious course was. And then the film-characters would delay a little longer, so that the audience fretted, since they knew what ought to be done, and no one would be doing it. And that was what suspense was all about, thought Gareth. A simple mechanism. Elizabeth would be impressed.

He glanced up at Elizabeth, ready to begin, when suddenly

  – ah the little knees –

made his eyes close and his heart pound. He sat back and after a few seconds gained control of himself.

Had she noticed, did I jump? I usually jump. He took another quick look at Elizabeth. No, she had not noticed. She held her loaded fork halfway between her lips and her plate, and in the flickering black-and-white her eyes glinted.

– its little papery knees –
Shut up and watch, watch!
Gareth watched.

'This is daft,' said Cissie, putting her cup down. 'You'd think they'd get the RAF in.'

'Shut up, Mum,' said Marion mildly. She wore her hair up in a small tight bun on the top of her head, and her pale-green going-away suit. The very tops of her ears, Jeff had noticed, were pink and peeling, as if from unaccustomed exposure.

'Did you miss the telly in Ibiza?' he asked her tenderly. She was different already, he recognized. All the visit long she had somehow spoken to Cissie as one married woman to another. He had indeed lost her through marriage, he thought sadly; but not to her husband: to his own wife.

'A bit,' said Marion. 'We went out a lot though. You know. Who's that?'

'A baddie,' replied Cissie. She sat on the sofa with her arms folded. Marion sat beside her, in the same pose.

'It was him told the plant-man about the pod in the Antarctic,' Cissie went on.

'What pod?'

'It ate the botanist. Grew into that thing 'cos the plant-man give it a beefsteak.'

Marion nodded. 'I see,' she said.

Joan sat shamelessly in her own chair, with her feet on Lily's footstool. 'Why don't you call in the RAF?' she demanded of the small glowing screen. 'Precision bombing, that's what they want,' she added, looking for agreement over at Lily's empty chair.

For a moment, remembering again, Joan abruptly was all extreme panic, as if she sat not in her own Dunnett Street front room but in the screaming fuselage of a last-second-but-one crashing aeroplane.

At first this sensation, which had visited often in the days following Lily's death, had made her gasp and groan aloud. This had so frightened and, eventually, annoyed everyone at the funeral that Cissie, feeling unable to concentrate properly over Joan's ghastly irruptions, had squeezed her sister's arm quite painfully just above the elbow and in fierce whispers ordered her to keep quiet.

Still keeping quiet Joan held onto the chair-arms until the sensation faded. After a few seconds she remembered Lily's crime, and felt much better.

On the screen the Krinoid, in a shower of bricks, was battering madly away at a stately home. What was it so bothered about? Why didn't it lumber away and hide in some nice safe wood? Clearly the luckless Krinoid's number would soon be up.

'Stupid thing,' said Joan to the Krinoid.

The title-music started up.

'Ron Grainger,' said Elizabeth from memory, 'and the BBC Radiophonic Workshop!'

'Correct,' said Gareth, reading from the screen. 'I suppose,' he went on, remembering his theory, 'you know *why* it's so exciting?'

'It isn't exciting. It's silly. I know it is. I just like it, that's all. I've been watching it since I was five and it's comforting to watch it now. So don't nag.'

'Was I? Nagging?'

Elizabeth smiled. 'Only a bit.' She put her fork down, and looked at him. 'Are you feeling better?'

'What?'

'Are you feeling better? You look a bit better anyway. You looked awful last week. I wish you'd tell me what it's all about.'

Gareth shrugged uneasily. 'I told you. My grandmother died. My mother's really upset. It's all been rather tense, that's all.'

Elizabeth shook her head. 'No. You're different. You've changed.'

Gareth thought he detected a little Hollywood, and felt he had a right to be slightly annoyed. 'For the better, I hope?'

'Yes,' said Elizabeth simply. 'Yes. It's very hard to explain. You just seem – chastened. Chastened. As if you'd been frightened. I keep thinking, What is it? What frightened him?'

Gareth pulled amazement-faces to hide his amazement. Elizabeth had often claimed unusual sensitivity to the feelings of others; claimed it rather too often, Gareth had always thought. Was there, after all, some basis for her vanity?

'I wish you'd tell me all about it,' she said again.

'So you could tell me what you'd have done differently?'

'What? What do you mean?'

'Nothing. No, nothing.' Gareth shook his head, and then looked up suddenly. 'D'you think you ever quote it?'

'Quote what?'

'Your addiction. Your programme. The one you've been watching for the last twenty years.'

'Quote it?'

'Yes. I was thinking, you see. That all our thoughts and reactions and so on, we think they're ours, spontaneous. But really they all stem from films and telly and so on. And it's very hard to tell what's your own and what isn't.'

Elizabeth was watching television. A future series was being promoted. 'Look,' she said, 'they're doing *The Diary of a Nobody*.'

'Elizabeth.'

'I heard, I heard. I expect it's true but it doesn't really matter, does it? Look how we all quote the Bible and

184

Shakespeare – and *Desert Island Discs*, all right, what does it matter?'

'But this is different.'

'What you mean is, it's all right to have your mental apparatus all cluttered about with bits of Shakespeare, but it's not all right to be cluttered about with bits of MGM. What's the difference? It's still clutter, isn't it? Our whole lives are a quote. We all do the same things and make the same mistakes. So what's wrong with quotation?'

After a pause Gareth reached out, undid Elizabeth's shoelaces, and tied her feet together.

Elizabeth watched. 'Now you'll have to do the washing-up.'

'It was my turn anyway,' said Gareth humbly.

Joan, picking up the tea-tray as the credits rolled, noticed the extra teacup and saucer and sighed. Done it again. Perhaps she would go on doing it for years, all her life; but then again, soon she would be setting up trays for when Dierdre popped upstairs.

'We can share the garden,' Dierdre had added when proposing the empty flat above her own.

What, with half your father in it? Joan had been tempted to exclaim. Then she had remembered that she herself had buried her half-sister in a sand-pit.

'We got a lot in common,' Dierdre had continued. Politely she had ignored Joan's answering burst of wild laughter.

'You could get a cat.'

'Pets allowed?'

'You know I've got two.'

'I'd like a cat. I'd like that.'

''Course it'd prefer me,' said Dierdre warningly. 'Cats always like me best.'

Joan, detecting Cissie-ism, was not impressed. It won't prefer her, she told herself determinedly. It'll like me best.

I'll get it very small, and be its mother. It'll like me best. A black cat, like Peterkin's on the Coral Island.

She picked up the *Radio Times*, put her feet back on Lily's footstool, and settled herself down again in her own armchair.

About her the house made its small night-time noises. If there were ghosts, Joan never heard them. Doors vibrated, soot pattered; Joan knew it was the wind.

Joan smiled to herself, and turned the page.

'Did you know,' asked Elizabeth, flourishing her tea-towel, 'that there's a statue in these parts, of Mr Pooter himself?'

Gareth laughed. He felt much better this evening.

'No, really,' said Elizabeth. 'Mr Pooter, rampant. Practically. Pointing at heaven. It's him all right.'

'Where?'

Elizabeth giggled. 'In the Mile End Road.'

'There's a statue of Mr Pooter in the Mile End Road?'

Elizabeth nodded. 'I'll show you tonight if you like.'

'I can't wait.' There might, thought Gareth, be a good story in that somewhere.

'What's your aunt going to do, anyway?' Elizabeth asked abruptly. 'The one that looked after your grandmother.'

'Oh, her. Going to live near a friend of hers, I think.'

'Poor thing. It's always the women, you know, who give up their lives like that.'

'She'll be all right.'

'What was she like, your grandmother? Did you know her?'

'Not really,' said Gareth, paling slightly. 'Except. Well. I don't think she was really cut out to be anybody's mother. She really wasn't the type.'

'Good job she didn't have much choice about it then, isn't it,' said Elizabeth, 'or you wouldn't be here at all.'

'I suppose so . . .' Gareth thought again of Lily choosing

186

her time to die, of Lily creating the only diversion great enough under the circumstances to allay all suspicion. He thought of the number of wash-cycles he had put his jeans through, and the number of times he had showered and washed the bath out, and the number of times imagination, taking a tip from brutal memory, had furnished him with a sarcastic Holmesian detective, running one bony, sensitive finger about the plug-hole, straightening up and demanding,

'And just how do you explain this, sir, please?'

'What is it, Officer?' croaked Gareth, again and again.

'Just a little, just a few grains of *sand*, Dr Williams!'

'What's the matter, Gareth?'

Gareth rinsed the cup he held. 'Nothing. Sorry. Miles away.'

'We'll go out then. See Mr Pooter?'

'Yes. Nice; a statue of Everyman. Makes a change.'

'Mm.' Elizabeth nodded. 'After all, he's usually dead, isn't he? Everyman, I mean. He's usually a dead soldier. Nice to see him rampant.'

Gareth, turning, gave her a kiss.

MORE ABOUT PENGUINS, PELICANS, PEREGRINES AND PUFFINS

For further information about books available from Penguins please write to Dept EP, Penguin Books Ltd, Harmondsworth, Middlesex UB7 0DA.

In the U.S.A.: For a complete list of books available from Penguins in the United States write to Dept DG, Penguin Books, 299 Murray Hill Parkway, East Rutherford, New Jersey 07073.

In Canada: For a complete list of books available from Penguins in Canada write to Penguin Books Canada Ltd, 2801 John Street, Markham, Ontario L3R 1B4.

In Australia: For a complete list of books available from Penguins in Australia write to the Marketing Department, Penguin Books Australia Ltd, P.O. Box 257, Ringwood, Victoria 3134.

In New Zealand: For a complete list of books available from Penguins in New Zealand write to the Marketing Department, Penguin Books (N.Z.) Ltd, Private Bag, Takapuna, Auckland 9.

In India: For a complete list of books available from Penguins in India write to Penguin Overseas Ltd, 706 Eros Apartments, 56 Nehru Place, New Delhi 110019.

A CHOICE OF PENGUINS

☐ *Further Chronicles of Fairacre* **'Miss Read'**   £3.95

Full of humour, warmth and charm, these four novels – *Miss Clare Remembers, Over the Gate, The Fairacre Festival* and *Emily Davis* – make up an unforgettable picture of English village life.

☐ *Callanish* **William Horwood**   £1.95

From the acclaimed author of *Duncton Wood*, this is the haunting story of Creggan, the captured golden eagle, and his struggle to be free.

☐ *Act of Darkness* **Francis King**   £2.50

Anglo-India in the 1930s, where a peculiarly vicious murder triggers 'A terrific mystery story . . . a darkly luminous parable about innocence and evil' – *The New York Times*. 'Brilliantly successful' – *Daily Mail*. 'Unputdownable' – *Standard*

☐ *Death in Cyprus* **M. M. Kaye**   £1.95

Holidaying on Aphrodite's beautiful island, Amanda finds herself caught up in a murder mystery in which no one, not even the attractive painter Steven Howard, is quite what they seem . . .

☐ *Lace* **Shirley Conran**   £2.95

Lace is, quite simply, a publishing sensation: the story of Judy, Kate, Pagan and Maxine; the bestselling novel that teaches men about women, and women about themselves. 'Riches, bitches, sex and jetsetters' locations – they're all there' – *Sunday Express*

A CHOICE OF PENGUINS

☐ ***West of Sunset*** **Dirk Bogarde**   £1.95

'His virtues as a writer are precisely those which make him the most compelling screen actor of his generation,' is what *The Times* said about Bogarde's savage, funny, romantic novel set in the gaudy wastes of Los Angeles.

☐ ***The Riverside Villas Murder*** **Kingsley Amis**   £1.95

Marital duplicity, sexual discovery and murder with a thirties back-cloth: 'Amis in top form' – *The Times*. 'Delectable from page to page . . . effortlessly witty' – C. P. Snow in the *Financial Times*

☐ ***A Dark and Distant Shore*** **Reay Tannahill**   £3.95

Vilia is the unforgettable heroine, Kinveil Castle is her destiny, in this full-blooded saga spanning a century of Victoriana, empire, hatreds and love affairs. 'A marvellous blend of *Gone with the Wind* and *The Thorn Birds*. You will enjoy every page' – *Daily Mirror*

☐ ***Kingsley's Touch*** **John Collee**   £1.95

'Gripping . . . I recommend this chilling and elegantly written medical thriller' – *Daily Express*. 'An absolutely outstanding storyteller' – *Daily Telegraph*

☐ ***The Far Pavilions*** **M. M. Kaye**   £4.95

Holding all the romance and high adventure of nineteenth-century India, M. M. Kaye's magnificent, now famous, novel has at its heart the passionate love of an Englishman for Juli, his Indian princess. 'Wildly exciting' – *Daily Telegraph*

KING PENGUIN

☐ *Selected Poems* **Tony Harrison** £3.95

Poetry Book Society Recommendation. 'One of the few modern poets who actually has the gift of composing poetry' – James Fenton in the *Sunday Times*

☐ *The Book of Laughter and Forgetting*
  Milan Kundera £3.95

'A whirling dance of a book . . . a masterpiece full of angels, terror, ostriches and love . . . No question about it. The most important novel published in Britain this year' – Salman Rushdie in the *Sunday Times*

☐ *The Sea of Fertility* **Yukio Mishima** £9.95

Containing *Spring Snow, Runaway Horses, The Temple of Dawn* and *The Decay of the Angel*: 'These four remarkable novels are the most complete vision we have of Japan in the twentieth century' – Paul Theroux

☐ *The Hawthorne Goddess* **Glyn Hughes** £2.95

Set in eighteenth century Yorkshire where 'the heroine, Anne Wylde, represents the doom of nature and the land . . . Hughes has an arresting style, both rich and abrupt' – *The Times*

☐ *A Confederacy of Dunces* **John Kennedy Toole** £3.95

In this Pulitzer Prize-winning novel, in the bulky figure of Ignatius J. Reilly an immortal comic character is born. 'I succumbed, stunned and seduced . . . it is a masterwork of comedy' – *The New York Times*

☐ *The Last of the Just* **André Schwartz-Bart** £3.95

The story of Ernie Levy, the last of the just, who was killed at Auschwitz in 1943: 'An outstanding achievement, of an altogether different order from even the best of earlier novels which have attempted this theme' – John Gross in the *Sunday Telegraph*

KING PENGUIN

☐ *The White Hotel* **D. M. Thomas** £3.95

'A major artist has once more appeared', declared the *Spectator* on the publication of this acclaimed, now famous novel which recreates the imagined case history of one of Freud's woman patients.

☐ *Dangerous Play: Poems 1974–1984*
   Andrew Motion £2.95

Winner of the John Llewelyn Rhys Memorial Prize. Poems and an autobiographical prose piece, *Skating*, by the poet acclaimed in the *TLS* as 'a natural heir to the tradition of Edward Thomas and Ivor Gurney'.

☐ *A Time to Dance* **Bernard Mac Laverty** £2.50

Ten stories, including 'My Dear Palestrina' and 'Phonefun Limited', by the author of *Cal*: 'A writer who has a real affinity with the short story form' – *The Times Literary Supplement*

☐ *Keepers of the House* **Lisa St Aubin de Terán** £2.95

Seventeen-year-old Lydia Sinclair marries Don Diego Beltrán and goes to live on his family's vast, decaying Andean farm. This exotic and flamboyant first novel won the Somerset Maugham Award.

☐ *The Deptford Trilogy* **Robertson Davies** £5.95

'Who killed Boy Staunton?' – around this central mystery is woven an exhilarating and cunningly contrived trilogy of novels: *Fifth Business, The Manticore* and *World of Wonders*.

☐ *The Stories of William Trevor* £5.95

'Trevor packs into each separate five or six thousand words more richness, more laughter, more ache, more multifarious human-ness than many good writers manage to get into a whole novel' – *Punch*. 'Classics of the genre' – Auberon Waugh